Leonora has managed to save her pregnant sister from a vampire attack, but to insure the safety of her sister and niece, Leo is willing to pay with everything but her life.

Covered in her own blood, she approaches the Mayor of Redbird City—who happens to be the local vampire king—and makes a deal. She will serve him as his assistant if he will keep her sister and niece from being torn apart.

Matthias agrees willingly to take on a new assistant and sends his men out to keep her sister safe. It is the beginning of a partnership that will make her his apprentice, send her to negotiate for dragons, visit crime scenes and keep her doing his bidding while her sister's attackers rally and prepare to try again.

Leo picks up her baseball bat and gets ready for the fight of her life.

The characters and events in this book are fictitious. Any similarity to real persons, living or dead, is coincidental and not intended by the author.

Copyright © 2016 by Viola Grace
ISBN: 978-1-987969-20-7

©Cover Design by Carmen Waters

All rights reserved. With the exception of review, the reproduction or utilization of this work in whole or in part in any form by electronic, mechanical or other means, now known or hereafter invented, is forbidden without the express permission of the publisher.

Published by Viola Grace

Look for me online at violagrace.com, amazon, kobo, B&N and other eBook sellers.

Defying Eternity
An Obsure Magic Book 5

by

Chapter One

Leo dropped off the last of her sister's exceptionally tipsy friends and made sure that Kat managed to get into her home with only a modicum of giggling and fumbled keys.

Leo had never suspected that a baby shower could have involved that much alcohol, but with her sister unable to imbibe, her friends took it upon themselves to consume what appeared to be the entire nine months' worth of booze.

Careful driving had saved her upholstery, but now that it was dark, she was happy not to see the sidewalks of the neighbourhood when she pulled back into her sister's driveway. There were some sights that no one needed to see twice. Two of the ladies had tried to race but had to stop when their stomachs protested. Leo was just grateful that the protest had happened outside her car.

She rounded her vehicle and brought out her present for her upcoming niece—a lovely alder wood bat with a big pink bow. Since her daddy had taken off, she was going to be depending on Leo to be her masculine example. It was a situation she was studying up for. Baseball seemed a good start.

She slammed the trunk and nearly missed the sound of breaking glass. Her sister's scream was harder to miss.

Leo sprinted into the house with the bat in her hands, going in through the back door with its shattered pane.

Minny's screams were deafening, but her tone was angry.

"Get away from me, you son of a bitch!"

In the living room, Leo saw a horror scene that she would never forget. Her sister was pinned to the ground, holding off her ex-fiancé. Robert was gnashing his newly sprouted fangs and trying to tear large holes in his pregnant ex.

"You heard the lady." Leo saw his eyes widen as she swung, but the bat caught him in the jaw and sent him backward.

Minny gasped and held her neck with one hand; the other was protectively over her belly.

Leo swung again and again, driving the vampire backward with strikes that had the desired effect. Finally, she was able to put herself between him and her sister.

Robert wasn't himself; he was some feral thing. She drove him back until he was cowering against the wall, the meaty strikes of the bat inflicting the damage she was aiming to create.

Clawed hands gripped her and pulled her away from her attack. She heard a scream and felt a bite, tearing at her neck and shoulder. Leo hissed but kept hold of her weapon as she was tossed aside.

A woman in tight pants and a tighter shirt bent

over Robert and lifted him. She glared at Leo as she turned with him in her arms. "This isn't over. She has to die."

"Not while I am around."

The creature smiled, her waxy-white skin glowed with a weird light. "I will simply have to do it when you are not at her side."

Minny groaned, and Leo grabbed the phone, dialling for help.

As silently as the woman had arrived, she was gone.

Leo went to her sister's side and looked at the damage. Minny wasn't going to be able to wait.

"Minny, hold tight. I am getting you out of here." She grabbed her sister and hauled her to her feet, ignoring the shriek of pain. She couldn't let Minny's pain take her over. She had to get her to the hospital.

Leo thanked her foresight for getting an SUV. The smoke-blue vehicle was the perfect height for her sister as Leo eased her into the front seat.

"I don't want to bleed on your upholstery." Minny gasped.

"Don't worry about it. Just hold tight. I am going to break some land speed records."

She started up her car, called the emergency line on the car phone and outlined her route. She was about to seriously break some speed regulations.

Minny's breathing became shallow, and then, she grunted. "Sorry, Leo. My water broke."

"Not a problem. No cop will dare detain us for this. If they do... damn. I left the bat at your place."

Minny chuckled, but it was obvious that she was getting weaker.

Leo watched for oncoming traffic and drove like the hounds of hell were on her tail.

She slowed carefully into the emergency cul-de-sac; the operator that she had chatted with during her riotous drive had warned a team with a gurney of their arrival.

"We were told there was only one woman injured." The man in the hospital scrubs scowled.

"There is; she is in labour. Her name is Minny. Blood type O positive. She is nine months along. She is due in three weeks, but the baby wasn't waiting."

She was babbling, but she couldn't stop it as they lifted the lifeless form of Minny out of the front of her car.

"Ma'am? You are injured as well."

She looked over at another young man, and she frowned. "Am I?"

"Yes, ma'am. It looks like a vampire attack."

"Oh, it was." She smiled weakly and slumped back, leaning on her car.

"I think you should come inside."

"I will just park, and then, I will be right there. You are taking good care of Minny?"

"We are. She is in the best of hands."

"Good. I will be right back." Leo nodded and straightened.

With deliberate concentration, she got back into her vehicle, started her car and drove out of the parking lot and toward the exclusive end of town.

Instinct and rumour drove her to the huge, silent house on the hill and the ten-foot wall that surrounded the massive property.

The security officer looked at her in surprise when she rolled down her window. "Yes, miss? What can I do for you?"

"Is the mayor available? I have an urgent vampire issue that I would like to discuss with him." Leo used her best administrative-assistant voice.

"Just a moment."

She waited and tried to fight off the grey edges that blurred her vision.

"Go on up to the house. Good luck."

She nodded, and the moment the gate swung open, she headed inside.

Her plan had formulated while she had driven to save her sister's life. There was only one way to fight a vampire, and that was with a bigger, scarier vampire. The Mayor of Redbird City would definitely fit the bill.

Leo parked carefully and got out of her car, holding onto the metal until the world paused its spinning under her.

She walked up the steps and into the huge mansion that contained the scariest and strongest vampire on their hemisphere.

A butler opened the huge and ornate door, letting her in without batting an eye. "He is waiting for you in his office. This way, please."

The man swung the door closed behind her and led the way down the hall until he opened another door for her. "Here you are, miss. Would you care for a towel?"

She smiled weakly. "Yes, please. Thank you. A glass of water, too, if that is not too much to ask."

"Of course, miss."

He stepped aside, and she passed him, walking into the peculiar stillness that meant an ancient vampire was near.

A high-backed chair shifted, and a deep voice rolled over her. "You have nerve, miss. Covered in blood, you come to a vampire. Are you bait, or do you need something?"

"Mr. Mayor, I have a vampire problem that I need your help with. My sister and niece are in danger, and I will do whatever it takes to keep them safe."

The chair turned slowly, and she was soon looking at a man she had only ever seen on news reports and in the papers.

His eyes widened in shock. "You have been bitten."

She snorted. "Torn up, more like. She was going for damage, not blood."

He was in front of her in less than a heartbeat, visually examining her wounds. "This is bad. How is it you are still standing?"

"I am motivated. I am not going to rest until Minny is safe."

"Minny?"

"Minuet Wicks and her daughter who was last named Cupcake, though I think she might have been supplanted by another favourite food."

"And you are?" He was so close, she could touch him by inhaling deeply, but her shirt was all bloody and his looked to be designer. She didn't want to damage it.

"Leonora Wicks. Administrative Assistant to the Acquisitions Director at the Redbird City Museum."

"Leonora. Well, you need to sit down, before you fall down, and tell me what happened."

"Can I just tell you from here? I think if I sit down, I will pass out and I don't want that.

"Very well."

"I will go over the details. It started six months ago when Robert decided that fatherhood wasn't for him. He disappeared, and we got the idea that he was Renfielding for a female vampire out of town, licking her boots on a regular basis."

Mayor Matthias raised his brows. "He knew he had fathered a child?"

"He knew. It was why he left."

"Ah. Continue."

"Everything was fine until tonight. I had moved in with my sister to help her with the baby prep, and I was coming back after being designated driver to all of her tipsy friends when I heard the scream." She shivered. It was a memory of hearing fury and fear rolled into one sound.

"What did you do next?"

"I ran in with the present I had for my niece. I never imagined it would come in handy."

He smiled slightly. "What was it?"

"A baseball bat. A nice alder bat that I had an artisan make for her."

"You fended a vampire off with a bat?" There was an impressed expression on his face.

"Yeah, it was going well until the lady came.

She is the one who attacked me, scooped Robert up and told me it wasn't over. I knew in that moment she wasn't going to rest until Minny was dead and the baby with her."

He tilted his head. "If the baby is born, he only needs to kill the child."

Fury ran through her. "No one is getting near her."

"And you would like help with that?"

"I would. I can offer you anything short of my life."

He raised his brows. "Really? It is hard to tell under all this blood, but you seem to be an attractive little thing."

She tried to work up outrage, but she was getting very tired.

"But, you also have a quick wit and an ability to act. That is a valuable set of skills. Are you a good assistant?"

She snorted. "I am one of the best. I have connections in a variety of locations and occupations and can make just about anything happen."

He nodded as if coming to a decision. "Well, in that case, your price will be to come work for me. The pay rate will be competitive and the bonuses are well worth the late nights that I occasionally require. Most of your skills will be at use during the day and briefings will be given to me after sunset. I can roam around during the day, but there is rarely a reason for me to do it."

"What will you do for Minny and the baby?"

"I will dispatch a series of guards to be with them around the clock. Shifters and others will keep your kin safe."

Leo looked into his eyes with their blood-red irises, and she nodded. "Deal. The moment they suffer an injury, I will be after you to see what it takes to kill you."

Matthias smirked. "I would enjoy seeing you try. Ah, Reed is here with some water and a towel for you."

Leo turned to look, but the movement was one too many for her. The slowly knitting skin on her shoulder tore open, and she fainted.

Chapter Two

Leo sat up and blinked, the smell of blood was gone. She looked down, and she was wearing a huge white button-down shirt with nothing under it.

The room had changed as well. The office was gone, and she was propped up on a chaise lounge with an intent goblin staring at her.

"Oh, hello." Leo smiled slightly.

The goblin nodded before getting up and leaving her.

Alone in the room, she touched the skin of her neck and shoulder. It was whole. Sensitive but whole. *How had that happened?*

A blur of motion warned her of his approach, and when Matthias was next to her, he smiled. "Welcome back to the land of the living, so to speak."

"How long was I out?"

"Two hours. I had the goblin lick your wounds closed. You will still be lightheaded, but you will be mobile. The hospital is waiting, and the XIA have been given your blood samples to track the vampires involved."

"I know who it was."

"And I am going through all official channels to keep the nest from getting up the nerve for a full-scale attack. If they know we are watching for them, they will keep to the shadows."

Leo nodded and swung her legs to the side. "Right. I need to get back to Minny."

"So, you have agreed to my terms? You will work as my assistant?"

She wrinkled her nose. "I am going to have to resign my current position at the museum."

"I will make a few calls. Take two days to be with your sister before you bring your possessions here to the manor."

Leo had been ready to stand, but she slumped. "I never said I would move in here."

"And yet you will. My assistants are normally vampires, and they are at my beck and call night and day. You want to fill that position? You will have to abide by the standards."

She made a face, and he chuckled.

"Leonora, I am offering you round-the-clock protection for your family. I expect the same from you in your service."

There was no doubting that it was a fair trade if it kept Minuet safe.

She pressed her lips together. "I agree. Fine. As long as I get to spend time with my family."

"We will come to an arrangement." He smiled wide, and his fangs were showing.

His expression was appallingly hostile, but she extended her hand to his. "Done."

He blinked and shook her hand, pulling her to

her feet in a rush.

She held onto him for a moment while her head settled. "Um, thank you."

His body wasn't like holding cool marble; it was like touching a mobile mannequin. There was some yielding to his skin but not much.

As soon as the spinning slowed, she stepped back. "I am heading to the hospital."

His hands were on her elbows. "Yes, you are. My car is waiting to take you. You are not fit to drive."

She scowled. "How will I get my car?"

He reached into his pocket and held up a phone. "My driver's number is in here and set for automatic dialling. Simply call him. As your sister's condition is at stake, I am sure that you will not wish her to be in any unsafe situations, like a regular cab."

Leo swallowed and looked into his pale eyes. "Right. Of course."

"Your shirt and bra were a dead loss, I am afraid. There wasn't time to provide you with proper replacements."

"Minny has seen me in worse."

"In that case, come this way." The mayor led the way through the halls, keeping one arm within her reach if she needed it.

She couldn't come up with a good excuse to grab hold of him, so she settled for walking slowly at his side, taking in the layout of the manor.

He led her out a side door where an exceptionally well-built man held the door of the dark sedan for her.

"Ms. Wicks, this is my driver, Nathaniel. He is at your disposal. Timorn and Limross will introduce themselves at the hospital." Matthias nodded with a small smile. "I will see you in forty-eight hours."

Leo looked to the driver. "What time is it?"

"Four in the morning."

"Right. Forty-eight hours from now. See you then, Mr. Mayor. Thank you again."

She slid into the car, and the door closed with a solid thunk. Nathaniel got into the front seat, and they were soon on their way.

The tinting on the windows made everything hazy, but she saw the gates as they left the mayor's manor, and the iron shut behind them.

Leo wanted to ask Nathaniel about how long he had worked for Matthias, but she ended up keeping her mouth shut. She was too tired for idle conversation, and she needed to focus on Minny.

Leo took the phone out of the shirt pocket, only to find that it wasn't a phone at all. It was a button and a small display screen.

"How does this work?"

The man didn't even glance at her in the mirror. "You push the button, and the countdown begins for my arrival. It means you will never wait in an unsecure area for me."

"Handy."

"Yes, Ms. Wicks."

She sat back and spent the rest of her journey worrying about Minny.

When they pulled up at the emergency room, Nathaniel got out and opened her door. He spoke to the emergency personnel that came out to greet them. "This woman is here to see her sister, Minuet Wicks. She has also suffered blood loss, and while her wounds are healed, she requires fluid."

Leo stepped out of the car, and she swayed. She had gotten up too damned fast.

The man in scrubs caught her by the arm and called for a wheelchair. Nathaniel spoke softly on his phone, and soon, there was another man in an expensive suit coming toward him.

The driver helped settle her in the wheelchair, and the other man in a suit took over.

"Ms. Wicks, I am Timorn, and I work for the mayor. I have been assigned as one of your sister's guards, and for now, I am going to put both of you in the same place."

The man in scrubs looked confused and tried to object. "She needs to be checked out."

"She can be, in her sister's room. I want them both where I can keep an eye on them. They are in danger, and the mayor wants them safe." He smiled tightly and pushed the wheelchair into the hospital.

He passed a number of staff members—who wanted to waylay them—took her up to the maternity floor and into a room guarded by another scowling man in a designer suit.

"Hello, Limross. I am Leo Wicks."

He smiled slightly and resumed his position as guard.

Timorn pushed her in next to a bed where Minny was bandaged up and on an IV. The monitor on her belly was recording the pulses of her body.

"Leo, you made it." Minny was relieved and tears started to fall.

"I did. I made it. No crying now. How are you feeling?"

Leo got out of the wheelchair and sat at the edge of Minny's bed.

Minny grabbed her hand. "I was so afraid you wouldn't make it."

Leo took in the bandages, the smears of blood on her skin and the hollow look in Minny's eyes. "I was afraid of the very same thing. Don't worry. Robert won't be able to get to you or the baby. You are safe. Timorn and Limross are here to protect you."

"So, I can have the baby?"

"You can have the baby."

Minny smiled. "Good. Can you catch it for me? It is coming."

To Leo's horror, Minny pulled her knees up and started pushing.

Leo looked at Timorn. "Call a doctor."

She steeled herself and walked to the end of the bed, lifting the sheet. The head of her niece was already firmly lodged in her mother's opening. Dark hair curled wildly, and the child slid forward.

Minny grunted and panted while she waited for the next contraction.

Leo listened to Timorn summoning medical assistance, but her focus was on the new relative that was squeezing its way into the world.

There was blood, there was liquid and Minny was shouting and grunting, but Leo focused and caught her niece.

Timorn came forward and whipped out a knife from somewhere. "I can cut the cord."

Leo glanced up as she eased her niece away from the pool of blood and other stuff. She lifted her up and placed her on Minny's chest. "Leave the cord until it stops pulsing. The blood is still being propelled to her for a reason. Like a butterfly plumping up its wings."

Minny chuckled and touched her daughter gently. "Leo did a lot of research on childbirth, just so she could nag the doctors in the delivery room."

It took a few minutes until the cord was ready to be cut, and by then, Leo had had to defend it from three different medical professionals. The placenta was delivered whole and intact, and Timorn shifted Minny to a clean bed.

The guards also refused to let the baby leave her mother's side.

Leo sat in her chair while she was finally given an IV of her own and a medical workup. With the excitement of the birth over, she looked at her sister and her new niece. They were definitely worth whatever price Matthias demanded she pay. Their safety was the only thing that was going to get her through the next eighteen years. Until the baby was grown and on her own, Leo was not going to have a relaxed moment.

At least Minny didn't know what she had done.

Chapter Three

"Are you insane, Leo? Linking yourself to a vampire is a deadly business." Minny sounded grumpy.

Leo jerked awake from her fitful sleep on her cot. "What?"

The tether jerked as she moved, and Leo looked at the tube that invaded her skin. She was on her second IV bag. Her body was thirsty.

"Timorn told me. He said that you had struck a deal with a vampire and that is why he and that other piece of man-candy are here."

"Limross and Timorn aren't candy; they are here to keep Robert from trying again."

Minny snorted and the baby sneezed. "They can't stay with me around the clock, Leo."

"No, they can't, but the other shifts can. I made the deal, and he is going to keep up his end."

"Who is it? All Timorn would say was that it was a vampire king."

"The only one I know. It is Mayor Matthias. I have just been hired to become his new assistant."

Minny blinked. "Is that a joke?"

"Nope. Have you decided on a name?"

"Melody Leonora Wicks. She gets nothing from Robert." She smiled and stroked the downy cheek of her child.

Minny sighed and held the baby out. "Okay, Mel, time to head over to Aunty Leo. She has had it too easy so far."

Aunty Leo stood up, took her IV pole with her and gained careful possession of her niece. "Hello, Melody. You gave your mommy all kinds of problems. Your name was almost Cupcake."

The baby stared at her with wide blue eyes, her lips pursed and relaxed. The dark curls made Leo smile. It seemed her niece took after her. The curls in the family were all hers.

Minny snorted. "Stop grinning. She looks like you. I agree. Unfortunately for you, she came out of me, and I am not letting you have dibs on her because of a resemblance."

"Well, with the new job looming, I don't see that it would be possible for me anyway. Do you know how long they are going to keep you?"

"A few more days. I am safe here; you can call off the guards."

Leo shook her head. "You are going to remain under guard until we take care of Robert and the woman who turned him into a vampire. Just little Melody existing is breaking their rules. No family. They can't have any family and belong to a nest."

"He decided that he wanted to pursue a chance at being a vampire right before I found out I was pregnant." Minny sighed. "He wants to kill Melody?"

"He doesn't even know her name, and he needs

her dead. I will find out what kind of clock he is up against, but until I am sure that no one will come after you, you will have guards around you twenty-four seven."

"What can two humans do against a vampire?"

Leo shrugged and handed the baby back to Minny. "We did a pretty good job, and we didn't even know they were coming. We were untrained, unprepared and unaware of what we were defending against. Oh, and the guys aren't human."

"What?"

"They aren't human. My guess is shifters. Limross looks feline, and Timorn looks like something with avian blood."

"How do you know that?" Minny sighed.

"You know me. I love to read. I worked at the museum for four years. I have seen my share of the extranaturals."

The door opened, and Limross poked his head in. "I am a panther; Timorn is an eagle. We both have excellent hearing." He pulled back, and the door shut.

Leo and Minny looked at each other for a moment and then giggled.

"When do you have to go to work?"

Leo made a face. "I have to move into the mayor's manor house at four in the morning in a day and a half. Wow, I should probably get free of the IV and start doing stuff, like clean up your place and get the baby kit so you can take her home."

"If your car is at the manor, how will you get home?"

Leo brandished the summoner. "With this."

She had to wait until the IV was disconnected, but the moment she was free, she pushed the button and the timer began its count down. She had seven minutes and twelve seconds.

Leo got a list of items that Minny wanted, and she took her leave of the guards.

There was three minutes on the clock, and it was just enough time to sign herself out and get to the lobby. She left the hospital with her head held high as the town car pulled up. Without missing a beat, Nathaniel got out and opened her door. She was tucked in, and they were rolling before she had given him the address.

"If I may ask, Ms. Wicks, how is your sister?"

Leo smiled. "A lot lighter than when she went in. My new niece is named Melody."

"Excellent. The mayor ordered your sister's home cleaned after the XIA had completed their investigation. The reason for the attack was self-explanatory, so they only needed to document the variety of blood before the cleaners came in."

"Where did they get the keys?"

"Your keys were in your vehicle. It is a habit to break. You should separate your domicile and vehicle by as much as you can."

Leo made a face at the back of his head. It was a tiny bit of rebellion that made her feel more like herself.

The guards around her sister's home were visible if you looked for them, and Leo was really looking.

"I will wait for you in the driveway."

Leo nodded. "Right. I will try and be quick."

"Of course." His head nodded.

The car pulled up, and she headed for the door, only then realizing that she didn't have her keys with her.

A shadow in the front yard moved, and a man with black hair slid forward. "Ms. Wicks?"

"Yes."

"I am Antony. I have been assigned to your sister's home." He extended her key ring with his left hand.

She nodded. "Thank you. Are you here all the time?"

"Yes. I am assigned to the house itself. Mayor Matthias is very eager to have you working for him, and you need to know that your sister and niece are protected."

"Did he read my resume or something?"

"Yes."

She was snickering as she went in and picked up the car seat, some baby clothes and wee little blankets to wrap Melody in. The baby bag was ready to go, so Leo grabbed that and lifted the entire collection into her arms. Antony helped her carry the stuff to the car. Leo stood and stared at the room where her sister and niece had nearly lost their lives.

"Matthias's people are very good at getting blood out of things. There was a surprising amount of vampire blood. The crew was impressed." Antony was behind her.

"That reminds me; I need my bat."

"It has been taken to the manor. It will be in your rooms."

She rubbed her hands together. "Right. Why was it taken to the manor?"

"Well, it was in your vehicle, so it was examined by the XIA and then returned to the mayor's possession."

"Why his possession?"

"He is acting as your legal proxy in this matter. When he asks for results, they generally appear. Are you ready?"

She nodded. "Yeah. I am just... yeah."

Leo turned and followed Antony to the car where Nathaniel was waiting.

"Back to the hospital, please."

"Yes, Ms. Wicks." Nathaniel closed the door and got behind the wheel.

Leo looked for Antony, but he had disappeared. She supposed that he was doing his job.

"Nathaniel?"

"Yes, Ms. Wicks?"

"How many people are on the protection detail for my sister?"

"Ten."

"Oh. Wow."

Nathaniel didn't say anything else. He didn't need to. It was a huge amount of folks to be posted just so that the mayor could get an assistant. Leo suddenly wondered what kind of work her position was going to entail.

"Thanks for bringing the baby bag." Minny chuckled.

"Not a problem. The house has been cleaned, and there is no trace of the attack. They even repaired that broken chair."

Minny blinked. "Wow. That is something. What did you do for them?"

"Nothing yet. That is what is making me a bit queasy. I am racking up quite a debt, and I have no idea what is going to be asked in payment."

Leo looked down at Melody and rocked her lightly. "Whatever he asks, it is worth it. This little miss is going to be completely safe. No vampire will get his hands on her."

Minny finished putting on her button-front shirt and smiled. "You also need to thank him for the goblin. I got all my wounds taken care of while you were out. I mean, it was a little creepy, but I get to go home today."

"He licked the wounds closed?"

Minny grinned. "Yeah. Do you know him?"

Leo chuckled. "We have met."

"He kept making faces. Apparently, the taste of plain and boring human is a little distasteful for him."

"I am not surprised. We are like eating dry toast in comparison to the extranaturals. Even little Melody here is untouched by the wave."

Leo wanted to bite back the word the moment she said it. The world was due for another wave of magic, and she didn't want Melody to be affected by it. She liked her niece all pink and human. Heck, she liked herself all pink and human.

Minny might look nice with pointed ears or maybe a fluffy tail, but Melody was perfect just as she was.

"So, they discharged you?"

"Yup, as soon as the goblin left. Do you know his name?"

Leo chuckled. "I don't even know if it is a him. It could be a woman."

"Yikes. That takes the licking to a whole other level." Minny chuckled. She set the car seat on the bed and wiggled her fingers. "Give me my offspring, Leo."

Leo lifted Melody high and walked over to Minny. "Well, Offspring is a fine nickname. You were nearly Cupcake, you know."

The baby flexed her little hands. Apparently, small pink people didn't care.

Minny tucked her baby into the car seat and fastened it. "Can you grab my bag?"

"Of course. Are we leaving?"

"We are. I just have to sign out and we are on our way."

"Okay. I will summon Nathaniel the minute you are done."

"You carry the bags; I have the baby."

"Let's go, sis. The sooner we get you home, the sooner I can get groceries laid in."

They exited the private room that Minny had been assigned. When they left the room, the guards fell in on either side.

Timorn didn't offer to take anything, but then, he shouldn't. As guards, they needed their hands free.

Minny went to the desk and signed out the baby. A wheelchair was brought to her. Apparently, it was hospital policy.

A fey nurse's aide pushed Minny and Melody

through the halls.

Leo summoned the car, and the clock was ticking at four minutes.

Leo noted the sweat trickling down the neck of the nurse's aide, so she stayed closer than she normally would have, and when Minny was shoved into the elevator where a pale woman was waiting, Leo jumped past the closing doors, Timorn at her side. The nurse's aide hadn't made it into the elevator.

When the pale woman reached for Melody with clawed fingers, a few things happened. Timorn shoved the stranger back against the wall, his head shifting into that of a huge eagle, snapping his beak at the vampire. Minny held the carrier tightly, and a pulsing aura started to emanate from her.

Leo hit the main-floor button and pulled the wheelchair as far back from the attacker as she could.

The blue wave washed through the small, moving space and held them all in place.

When the chime announced their arrival, the bubble popped. Leo pushed her sister out of the elevator, and the door closed on Timorn and the chalky woman.

Limross was waiting for them, unruffled and not a hair out of place.

Leo checked the time on the summoner and exhaled slowly. "He will be here in a minute."

Limross nodded. "Timorn will deal with the attackers here. My duty is to get you home."

Leo followed him to the exit where the car was pulling up.

Minny got to her feet, cradling the baby in the carrier. "We have a car and driver?"

"My car is still at the manor. Nathaniel is an excellent driver, and he will get us home safely." Leo was talking to Limross as well as Minny.

Leo wasn't wrong. Nathaniel was waiting. He opened the door, took the baby carrier and placed it rear facing on the back seat in a matter of seconds that spoke of previous practice.

The bags went into the trunk, Leo and Minny were tucked in, and Limross was in front next to Nathaniel. They left the hospital behind, and Leo couldn't even imagine what was coming next.

Chapter Four

"So, they tried to kill me. At the hospital."
"No, they tried to kill Melody. She is the one trace of Robert's bloodline that is surviving. For him to be able to be a vampire of any kind of standing, she has to die."

Leo smiled as Minny settled the carrier on the couch, and she held her baby in her arms again.

Limross was guarding the door, and Leo could see flickers of Antony outside. Whatever he was, he was guarding them.

"Melody. She did a weird thing in the elevator."
"That was her? I had hoped it was you."
"Nope. It was the baby. Look how hard she is sleeping now. It must have tuckered her out. Do you know what it was?"
"It was a temporal field. The clocks stopped and our bodies were locked in place. As defenses go, it was pretty impressive."
"How do you know that?"
"I was holding a timer, and the timer paused while we moved down the six floors. That is why Nathaniel was already there when the timer said we had a minute."

"Yeah, but how do you *know?*"

"I have worked at the museum for a few years now. It is my job to know the exhibits and that means doing the research before we do any of the fundraisers. I have to know more than the docents when it comes to the installation, and that includes the first signs of magic in our world."

Leo chuckled and took the laundry to the basement. "Temporal magic is one of the basics."

She left Minny muttering about her know-it-all sister and informing Melody that Leo was always to be listened to, but rarely to be trusted. Aunty Leo was smart and that was a very sneaky thing.

Leo grinned and washed the bloody clothing in cold water. If this was her last day with her sister, she was going to make it as normal as possible.

They ordered takeout, and that was when Leo had to explain about the guards. Antony had stopped the delivery person and taken the pizza and garlic bread. When he delivered it to the door, it was time for introductions.

"Minuet Wicks, this is your household guardian, Antony. He is posted at the house and is here to keep you safe, also, apparently, to scarf your pepperoni!" Leo lunged forward and yanked the open box from Antony's hands.

Minny was feeding Melody, and she smiled at the stranger. "Well, if you could come over here, I could shake hands with you. I am not particularly mobile right at this moment."

Antony stepped in and bowed over Minny's hand. "It is an honour to watch over you."

Minny's eyes gleamed. "She is busy eating, but this is Melody."

Leo blinked. Well, her sister had always been the more hot-blooded of the two of them, as was evidenced by Melody. Antony had similar sharp and handsome features to Robert, so he was Minny's type.

Leo set the pizza on the table and got some plates. "Antony, ask Limross if he wants pizza."

It was blissfully normal. Leo set out the plates and cups, and the guards had a meal before returning to the exterior of the home. Night was falling and vampires loved to hunt in the darkness.

If Robert was going to come tonight, he was in for a bit of a surprise.

Minny dozed off on the couch, so Leo took over with Melody. She changed her diaper and put her in the crib that had been set up before the baby shower.

The baby monitor took a bit of figuring out, but when it was next to Melody and recording her soft snuffling, Leo felt better.

She got Minny's bed ready and stroked her forehead. "Honey, wake up. You need a proper night's sleep."

Leo got her arm under her sister and hauled her up. Minny staggered, but Leo got her into bed, took off her shoes and tucked her in. She could sleep in her clothes.

She brushed Minny's hair away from her face and smiled softly. "It is definitely worth it."

Minny opened her eyes slightly, smiled and went back to sleep.

Leo straightened, went over to Melody's crib and stroked her downy cheek. The monitor was working, so Leo left the room and headed to her small room to start packing.

The small, snuffly noises from the monitor clipped to her jeans made her smile. She took the suits and blouses out of her wardrobe and zipped them into a few garment bags. Her t-shirts, socks, underwear and jeans all got crammed into duffel bags along with her sensible work heels and extra sneakers.

She kept out one change of clothing for the next day and headed to the kitchen to tidy up. There was something unsettling about the idea of sleeping while Minny and Melody were vulnerable.

When everything was neat and squared away, she checked on her family again before going outside and into the back yard. The wide swing called to her, and she settled on it in the dark, swinging gently. She took in the night around her and smiled when Melody started wailing. The muttering and mumbling was Minny's voice, and soon, there were soft sucking noises that explained the crying.

She felt her companion before she saw him. "Hello, Antony."

"Hello, Ms. Wicks." He appeared out of the darkness and leaned against a nearby tree.

"May I ask what you are?"

"Ah. Of course. I do give off confusing vibes. I am a dryad or the male version. A wild man of the woods."

"So, you just hang out in the woods?"

"I cast my mind into every growing thing, every blade of grass, every tree. I can feel anyone approaching the moment they leave the asphalt or concrete. Even then, if they are wearing hard-soled shoes, I can feel them coming."

She felt a little bit better about leaving her sister in his care. "Do you sleep?"

"No. The green space feeds me; light sustains me. The pizza was nice but not necessary."

"Then ask next time."

He grinned. "I would have, but it has been so long since I have been able to interact with normal humans that I behaved as normally as I could."

Leo smiled. "Do you know how long you will be assigned here? I don't want to get all dependent on you being here and then have you transferred away."

"Matthias ordered me to remain here for the duration of your employment with him. If you are with him, I will be watching over Minuet and Melody."

It felt good to hear him say it out loud. She smiled at him. "It is nice to know."

"Are you sure that you know what you are getting into with the mayor?"

She smiled slightly. "I know that I would do anything for those two in there. This is nothing compared to the pain I would inflict if anything were to happen to them. I would be broken, and then, I would go out until I got myself and a lot of other people killed."

"You are human."

"Humans were killing each other before the

wave. Magic doesn't have any exclusivity on homicide."

He inclined his head. "True. Now, go to sleep. Limross and the others will keep watch with me."

Leo smiled and got to her feet. "Good point."

Her bed was calling, and she set her folded clothing on a chair before stripping and crawling between the sheets. The knowledge that those who were willing to keep her niece safe surrounded the house was all she needed.

"I can't understand why he wants you to live in." Minny was swaying slightly with the baby in her arms.

"He keeps odd hours. While he can go out in daylight, he prefers not to or so the internet would have me believe." Leo winked and finished loading up the second diaper bag. She wanted to make sure that Minny was okay until she could get back for a visit.

"When will you have a day off?"

"I have no idea. I will hash out the details when I get there." Leo cleared her throat. "Since I won't be living with you, how would you feel if I hired a live-in nanny to help you?"

"Where would you get the money for that?"

Leo sighed. "I have some savings. I was going to buy a new car, but this seems a much better use of my funds."

Tears started in Minny's eyes. "I can't let you use all your money for me. You are already selling yourself."

"I am not hooking. I am renting myself for a finite amount of time. The same thing I do every day." She chuckled at the truth of it.

She had talked with her boss today, and he had informed her how happy he was to wish her luck on her new position with the mayor. Apparently, the museum was getting a lot of ancient documents on the origin of vampires in the next month.

Not knowing what she was in for when she started work, she dressed for the office. It was three in the morning, and it was time for her to summon the car. Her vehicle was still at the manor.

The rest of her clothing had been picked up that afternoon. The only thing that she had to bring to her new job was herself.

"I am going to call for Nathaniel. Will you be all right?"

Minny came over and handed Melody to her. "One big hug from Aunty Leo, and then, she can leave in peace."

Leo smiled and cuddled her niece. The warm body and smell of baby powder was a focal point that she wanted to remember. She was jumping into a world that she had no control over to keep this little one alive and healthy. It was a jump she was going to make every day for as long as it took to keep her safe from Robert.

After ten minutes of cuddling, Leo set Melody down in her bassinette, and she hugged Minny. "I will let you know how my first day at work goes."

"I expect to hear all the juicy details."

Leo leaned back and gave her a look that told her to get serious.

"I know, I know, you are always the soul of discretion."

Leo grinned. "It is not a bad thing to be known for."

Without looking, she reached into her pocket, pulled out the summoner and pressed the button.

Minny sighed. "You are sure that Robert is still out there?"

"Definitely. There would have been a notice for me if he were dead."

It would also have appeared on the news. New vampires had to be recorded and monitored. A loose or dead offspring would bring shame to its maker.

She checked the timer and inhaled. A minute to prepare to start a new job. Leo smiled at her sister. "Everything will be fine."

Chapter Five

The car glided to a halt in front of the manor doors.

Nathaniel gave her a whisper of encouragement. "Welcome to the team."

Leo put on her work face, walked up the steps and entered through the door that the butler held open for her. "Thank you, Reed."

He looked surprised. "I am surprised you remember me, miss. You were not in very good shape when you were last here."

"I remember everything that happened while I was awake." She smiled. "I believe I am to start work now?"

"Yes, miss. This way. He is definitely expecting you."

"Thank you." Once again, she was led through the halls, but this time, she could appreciate the artwork and the ringing sound of her heels on the stone floor.

Her business dress was knee length and a sober grey. She would be completely unremarkable in any boardroom in the country. Her hair was scraped back in a bun, and she had her unapproachable expression in place. It was the best way to start her workday. It felt so good to let her hair down after she was done for the day.

She swallowed nervously as Reed opened the door to Matthias's office. She really hoped that her face didn't show what she felt.

The vampire king who had been elected Mayor of Redbird City was bent over his desk and looking through a stack of reports.

She stepped forward and Reed disappeared. Positioned in front of the desk, she watched as the clock behind him ticked over to four o'clock.

The moment the time had struck, Matthias looked up with a smile. "You are on time. Excellent. It is a good start. Now, go through all of these and sort them by what needs to be attended to immediately while I get something to drink."

Leo looked at him in surprise, and when he gathered up the documents, walked around the desk and dropped them in her arms, she was speechless.

"Your desk is against that wall. Your computer, phone, tablet and pager are all there, as is your employment contract. Nathaniel is still at your service. I will be up for a few more hours if you have any questions."

She turned and headed to the desk with its delicate filigree carving. It looked like it was made of lace with a smooth granite top.

She dropped the paperwork he had handed her, and she turned on her computer with the login and password from the small sticky note attached to the cover.

Defying Eternity

The mayor's schedule was on the desktop, and she quickly familiarized herself with what he did and when he did it. Most of his activities were nocturnal, but there were a few meetings in the afternoons.

Some of the meetings had a small star on them, and she was going to have to ask about them.

With her immediate need for knowledge satisfied, she turned to the pile of paperwork. After half an hour, she paused to send a quick text to Minny to give her the work cell phone number.

When her sister had been contacted, she continued looking through the petitions and contracts as well as research information that folks were sending to the mayor.

She had three distinct piles worked out by the time he returned to the office.

Leo was onto her own contract and reading all that it entailed. Well, with the rate he was going to pay her, she could afford a nanny on her own. She smiled.

"What was that smile for, Ms. Wicks?"

She smoothed her features. "Apologies, Mr. Mayor. I was just thinking about hiring a nanny to help Minny with the baby. I had always planned to be there for her, but as matters have changed, it is time to make a new plan."

"I am glad you can adapt. Do you prefer a male or female nanny?"

"It doesn't matter as long as they are well versed in infant care and very reliable."

He nodded and picked up his phone. To Leonora's horror, he ordered a nanny like she ordered pizza—efficiently and with expectation of immediate delivery.

"Is that going to add more time to my service to you?"

"That is up to you. I will provide you with safety for your family until the date that it is no longer required."

From her desk, she had to ask, "Why me?"

"You took on a vampire queen and her newest offspring with a pregnant woman and a baseball bat. After that, you drove your sister to the hospital and then yourself here to point out to me that my local vampires were behaving in an unseemly manner."

He smiled at her. "You are a very impressive human. It is a rare thing and will throw off those that I do business with."

"So, I am a collectible?" She raised her brows.

"Indeed. Unique in my experience and that encompasses thousands of generations."

"You have to have met other people who did stupid stuff."

"Yes, but never with the calculated thought that you put into your reaction to the situation. You thought, reacted and operated with no calculation of your own survival in the equation. You committed before you could think and that is a definite asset to my team."

"It is funny how everyone refers to it as a team."

She took the different stacks of paperwork and got up from her desk. Leo walked over to him and handed him her contract.

"I would prefer to make the arrangements for a

nanny myself."

Matthias arched his brows. "I have already made the arrangements."

She frowned. "That is not necessary."

"Yes, it is. I will put it on your tab." He winked.

"At this point, I will have to work for you for two decades before I pay this off."

He shrugged. "That is a flicker of time for me."

She was aghast. "It is my niece's entire trip to adulthood."

"You don't say?" His lips curled in a smile.

Her fingers clenched on the paperwork. "When will I get to see her?"

"You will have one day off per week. It will depend on the schedule." He folded his fingers together and propped his chin on them.

"Speaking of the schedule, what do the stars mean?"

"Ah, those are meetings that you must accompany me. Now, what have you done with that paperwork?"

She frowned and got back into work mode. "Right. This bunch is infrastructure renewal. The two with flags on them are the urgent ones. The rest of the requests can be delayed without any damage to your approval ratings."

"Fascinating. Thank you. How long can they be delayed?"

"Into next quarter. In the fall, you will need to have the snow clearing ready, but you don't need it in the summer. You do need the potholes filled."

He smiled. "Excellent. What is next?"

She handed him the next pile of requests for

personal appearances. "The ones with flags do not conflict with your existing schedule, and the ones with two flags would help you with your appeal to the humans and extranaturals who live standard lives."

They went through the letters of critique, the invitations from other mayors and vampire kings, and finally, she was able to take the documents that were rejected and return to her desk, writing up polite letters declining the meeting, goods or services.

Reed brought her in a tray with a sandwich, a bowl of soup and some tea. "Here you are, Ms. Wicks. I am going off shift soon, but Dorn will be in to meet you and take you to your quarters when you need to change for the day."

She nodded. "Right. I am the day shift."

"Well, the deputy mayor and his assistant will be in shortly, so you need only worry about the documents you have already been assigned." Reed smiled and inclined his head.

"So, there is a different set of tasks for night and day?"

"Yes. The deputy mayor only appears at events and in conferences when they cannot wait for the mayor."

Leo pulled the reference out of her memory. "Able Rickman is the deputy mayor."

"Correct."

"And he is a zombie."

"Correct, as is his assistant, Mr. Crombie."

Leo kept a straight face with effort. Crombie the zombie was just too easy. "I am sure I will enjoy meeting them."

"I am glad you have confidence. Good morning, Ms. Wicks."

"Good morning, Reed." She smiled at him and kept typing a polite letter to indicate that the mayor would not be attending the sixteenth birthday of the untransformed werewolf daughter of the local pack. It had been in the schedule-conflict pile of documents.

She checked her schedule to see if she was required that evening, and it was free. She added a line that if they wanted the mayor's assistant in attendance to carry his regards, she was available.

Leo didn't know why she put that sentence on the document, but she printed it off on the heavy paper and set it on his desk with a signature flag before she could change her mind.

Three hours after she started, she was ready to take a rest. Her desk was clear, her phone was in her purse and the laptop was tucked under her arm when she left the office.

She looked to the left and right before she walked down the hall in search of Mr. Dorn.

For such a large man, he moved silently. Apparently, the day shift was a giant.

"Ms. Wicks?"

"Yes, good morning, Mr. Dorn."

"Just Dorn. This way to your quarters." He walked past the office and deep in to the manor house.

Leo followed him.

"The number to the kitchen is marked on your phone. If you are awake, food will be brought to you every four hours. The mayor does not eat, so you will get authorization to eat in his presence."

Leo snorted. *I will see about that.*

"During your monthly bleed, you will be asked to work from your quarters."

Dorn was walking slowly, but she still had to trot to catch up.

"Wow. Can I get time off?"

"No. You still have your duties. You will simply execute them from your chambers."

"Are there any other women here?"

"No. No other females live here. Frankly, when the mayor first mentioned you as Leo, I thought he was hiring another male assistant."

She quirked her lips. "I get that a lot."

"Your clothing has been unpacked and arranged. New work wear has been ordered for you based on your sizes, and you are to report to the mayor's office at midnight every night unless you have accompanied him to a meeting. Your schedule will be dictated by his."

"Of course. That is why I am here."

Dorn looked a little perplexed by that. He led her down a quiet hall and opened the third door from the end. "Here you are. Everything you require is inside your quarters. Good day."

"Good day." She stepped past him and into her room. The door closed behind her, and she whistled softly. The space was larger than the floor plan for Minny's house.

She put her computer and purse on the bedside table and checked out the bathroom. It was big enough for her to host a sleepover.

She glanced over at the tub, the white marble sink and the shower with enough heads in it to have a starring role in off-colour porn. She wouldn't be cleaned so much as assaulted.

The toilet was blissfully non-threatening.

She washed her hands, splashed her face and returned to her room to send Minny a text. When she got an answer, she sighed in relief. Everything was fine, baby was sleeping.

Leo checked her schedule and walked into her closet. Next to her modest clothes were a selection of work dresses that were in a variety of colours, all brilliant and attention getting. They were definitely not what she was used to wearing. Leo grabbed another bland dress.

She steeled herself and took a two-minute shower that woke her up, all over. When she was towelling off, she was pretty sure that she and the shower heads had just entered a weirdly intimate relationship.

Her hair was damp, so she let it down, brushed it out and braided it tightly. One day, she was going to cut it off, but until then, it was bondage all the way.

She got dressed, switched shoes and opened her laptop. The map of the manor was an embedded file, and she spotted the deputy mayor's office.

Introducing herself seemed like a good use of her time. She was on the clock until five in the evening.

Chapter Six

Leo walked with her head high and her new phone in her hand. Her clicking heels were the only sound in the halls.

In a city inhabited only by humans, the mayor would have been in the city hall. Here, communication was still done by letter and meetings were conducted face to face. Having their offices at the manor made sense when they would only connect with folks by appointment.

Leo had worked with exclusive companies before, but this took it to a whole new level.

The door to the deputy mayor's office was open, but she paused and knocked on the inside of the open door.

A man at a desk similar to hers looked up and smiled. "Yes?"

"Hello. Mr. Crombie?"

He smiled brightly for a man with grey skin. "Indeed. Oh, are you Ms. Wicks?"

"I am. I thought it would be a good idea to introduce myself."

The man at the main desk had golden hair that contrasted with his silvery skin. "Ah, so you are the young lady who has Matthias so excited. Well, for him." He chuckled.

"I don't know about that, but I am his new assistant. Tell me, is there anything I should know?"

Able, Dexter and Leo had a charming conversation that took up the rest of her shift. Dexter showed her the programs she needed as well as the information database on all extranaturals living in the city. It would do her good to learn what she needed to as quickly as possible.

She was walking down the hall toward her room when a familiar voice spoke.

"I thought you would be in bed by now."

She turned and smiled at Matthias. "First day at work is always rough. I was just turning in."

He inclined his head. "Make sure you tell the kitchen when you are awake."

Leo snorted. "Trust me; I have no problem finding food."

He grinned and flashed his fangs. "Me too."

She burst out laughing, inclined her head and headed back to her room.

"See you at midnight."

His voice reverberated through the hall. She got the feeling that he would be in her room if she wasn't in the office. That wasn't creepy at all.

She was going to sleep tight tonight.

The annoying buzz of her phone alarm got her out of bed, and she staggered to her bathroom without turning on the lights.

Brushing her teeth was a habit that she didn't

want to lose, no matter the time that she woke up.

Leo grabbed another shower and wrapped herself in a towel as she returned to her closet. "Son of a bitch."

She turned on the lights just to make sure that she was seeing what she thought she was. All of her boring dresses were gone. Someone had come in while she was sleeping and hijacked her clothing.

Leo grabbed the dark-red dress and stalked over toward her underwear drawers. When she looked at the neatly matched bra and panty sets, she screamed.

She spent the next ten minutes muttering and stalking around her quarters. If she admitted it to herself, the clothing was comfortable and the underwear was a good fit. Even the shoes were pretty, though higher than she wore for most workdays.

She had ten minutes left, and she hadn't eaten. *Damn it.*

Leo looked at the phone and decided that she could make it through the next four hours without a snack.

She grabbed a glass, filled it with water and gulped it down. That should hold her.

She grabbed her phone, her computer and her nerve and left the huge space that she had been allocated. Work waited.

Reed brought her a tea tray with some toast and tsked at her. "You should have eaten."

"I was distracted by the disappearance of my

wardrobe."

Reed looked a little embarrassed. "Mayor's orders. You represent him when you are seen in public, so he wished you to look your best."

She looked over at Matthias, and he smiled benignly. She lifted a triangle of toast and wedged it into her mouth before chewing savagely.

His shoulders were shaking.

Reed looked between them, and understanding finally dawned in his eyes. A slight smile played around his lips as he left the office.

"When you are finished with your tea, you will accompany me to a club opening."

She nearly choked on her toast. "There isn't a star on it."

"I am aware, but you seem to want to engage the community, and this will definitely let you see them and they see you."

Leo snarfed down the rest of her toast, poured a cup of tea and blew on it to cool it.

"So, Leonora, how did you sleep?" Matthias glanced at her.

"Like a rock." She sipped at her tea and got the first cup down with only mild discomfort in her throat.

She diluted the second cup of tea with some cold water from the pitcher on her desk, and it went down easy.

The paperwork was already finished. Apparently, yesterday, she had worked herself through a backlog.

"You have an artful turn of phrase when it comes to rejection documents. I believe that no one has been turned down as graciously in the last century."

She set her teacup down. "Sorry. I have a long history of being able to weave bullshit into fine silk."

He snickered again. "So I was led to believe. Apparently, your previous boss was not lying in order to gain my collection."

"The director is scrupulously honest for a man with his level of greed. His goals all involve improving and expanding the museum. Nothing else matters."

"Excellent. Very straightforward then. I will have you vet the collection before it is sent, just so I have a bargaining chip for any future favours."

"Did you promise anything specific?"

"No, just a few treatises on the origin of the vampires. We came into being after a wave but not in the way most folks think."

"The given and taken."

"Correct. Well, are you ready?"

She picked up her phone and was reaching for her purse when he said, "Check the desk drawer."

She opened the drawer and found a designer purse. It looked like it cost more than her car.

She pinched the bridge of her nose. "Why is there a designer bag in my desk? Is it hiding?"

"It is more appropriate to your new position. Gather it and let's go. Nathaniel is waiting."

He shrugged into a suit jacket, but her sleeveless sheath dress was going to have to do. At least the dark-red fabric was thick enough to keep her from feeling the night air.

She grabbed the new handbag, slipped in her

phone after checking that it had a full charge and got to her feet.

"What is the protocol when we are out in public?"

"You remain at my left side. When someone asks for an appointment, you check the schedule and make a note."

"Okay."

They were on the move toward the door.

"If it is necessary to introduce you, I will do so. If I offer my hand, take it."

She nodded and looked up at him. "How is it that a man born so long ago is your height?"

She could feel the tiny pause in his steps before he said. "I will tell you in the car."

Nathaniel was standing next to the open car door. He made a small gesture that told Leo to get in first. When Matthias piled in after her, she scooted to the far side.

It wasn't graceful, but she managed to perch on the passenger side with her knees together.

She buckled up out of habit. "So, was it rude of me to ask about your height?"

He chuckled. "No, it simply caught me by surprise. No one has asked about me in a very long time. I am guessing no one has dared."

"Of course."

"The reason for my height is the means by which I became what I am. Have you read the old myths on vampires?"

"About being bitten by bats? Yes."

"That is incorrect. The true story involves an ailing village, two brothers and the tree of life."

"That is a myth."

"It is now; it wasn't then." He smiled slowly. "When I was growing up, it was the ultimate source of life and survival. It would appear only to those who needed it, and when plague ravaged my village, I needed it. The change came from there."

There was a lot more to it, but that was as much as she was going to get.

"The club we are going to caters to the blood-drinking set. The name is Sanguine, and it will be best if you remain close to me."

Her stomach flipped. "Seriously?"

"Seriously. You are my contract employee but are not yet marked as being under my protection."

"What would that entail?"

He turned toward her, and his smile was slow as he looked at her with eyes that said he could see through her dress and he liked it. "More than you are wanting to give... for now."

"I have to give something?"

"Indeed. Given vampires do nothing without consent."

"Ah. Wow. That is news."

He snorted. "Prepare to be educated."

Nathaniel cruised through downtown, approaching a large crowd on the sidewalk. He pulled up and left the vehicle, opening the door next to Matthias so that the vampire could leave.

Lights flashed as pictures were taken. To Leo's amazement and embarrassment, Matthias extended his hand to her. She slipped her hand in his, tucked the handles of her bag over her arm and slid across the seat and out of the car.

Defying Eternity

He gave her an approving nod and lifted her to her feet.

She moved into place at his left and kept her face stony and her gaze forward as they walked into the club through a path lined with bouncers.

The crowd was made up of every nocturnal extranatural that Leo had ever read about. She tried to keep calm, but she knew her heart was pounding too fast. It was attracting predators.

Damn, she wanted her bat.

"Easy, Leonora. You will be fine." Matthias murmured it to her.

She kept her face blank and tried to embrace her inner calm. The owners came up to thank the mayor for his appearance, and Leo was drawn into the club with the rest of the bloodsuckers.

Leo sat next to Matthias and made appointments as he took requests from those who approached him. When he was in deep conversation with another very old vampire, she got up to use the rest room.

The trip to the ladies' room was uneventful, but as she left the hallway to return to Matthias's side, an iron hand wrapped around her arm and pulled her into the embrace of a very cold and very predatory vampire.

"Hello, cutie. You must be very brave to be here with all of us big, bad vampires."

She didn't respond, merely looked at him with her most impassive glare. "I am expected elsewhere."

He dragged a hand up and down her arm. "They won't miss you for a while. I only want a taste."

She heard the growl a moment before a hand

grabbed the man's face and the cracking of bones was heard.

Leo staggered free as Matthias stood over her suitor, and he wiped his hands off on a proffered handkerchief. The club owner was babbling apologies and holding a basin of water out for Matthias to wash his hands.

The vampire on the floor moaned and started twisting. Leo felt marginally better that he was alive.

Matthias looked at her. "Are you all right, Leonora?"

"I am fine. I was wishing for my bat."

He scowled. "That would have been more of a mess. He has learned manners and will not approach you again."

The vampire was being helped to a sitting position, and his face was slowly realigning.

"Come on, Leonora. There are more who wish to make appointments."

Leo followed him back to the half-circle seat and sat next to him once again. It was going to be a very weird night.

Chapter Seven

Vampires were excellent dancers. Their physical status made the most acrobatic moves look effortless.

Two hours into their visit, the owners had brought her noodles and chopsticks so that she wouldn't get her phone messy. Leo appreciated the gesture. No one else in the club was eating. Well, no one was eating food. There were a few consuming each other.

"You are handling this well." Matthias murmured it to her during a lull.

"I have seen a bit of these events in the video clips that Dexter gave me. There is a lot more moaning in person."

His shoulders shook as he looked over the alcoves and couches where the vampires were feasting on each other or willing participants.

Leo shrugged and ignored them.

"You don't find it fascinating?" Matthias was still amused.

"It is their business. Their bodies and their urge for public orgies. I am hoping that this place is licensed for that because that is all kinds of health violations."

"You raise an interesting point. Daniel!"

The male owner was at his side in a blur of pale flesh.

"While the blood sharing may be enjoyed here, the public sex is still an infringement as long as this is a public-access business."

Daniel blinked, looked around and was breaking up the fucking in seconds. The triad wasn't happy about it, but clothing was replaced and they headed for the dance floor to engage in fully clothed foreplay.

Leo sighed and watched the dancers. She didn't want to engage in the lewd behaviour, but dancing had always been something that haunted her dreams. She sucked at it. Her inability to let someone else lead meant that toes were stepped on and collisions were inevitable.

"Do you want to dance?"

She blinked. "Want to, yes. Will, no." Leo smiled tightly at Matthias.

"I believe I will have to make it an executive order then. Come with me."

He held out his hand, and she winced but placed her palm against his.

"I am a very bad dancer."

"I will take my chances. I have suffered much more than bruised toes in my day and survived it all."

She was hauled to the dance floor, and at the mayor's nod, a slow song began to play.

Leo swallowed as he pulled her against him, one hand at the small of her back and his other hand holding hers. She put her hand on his bicep as he steered her around to the slow saxophone wail.

"You are doing very well, Leonora."

"You, too. This isn't nearly as painful as I remembered." She blurted it out, but it didn't matter, he swayed with her around the dance floor. Other couples gave them a wide berth, but this time, she knew it was about Matthias and not her.

When the song finally faded away, he led her back to the couch and the requests for appointments began again.

Leo could see when dawn was approaching. The packed club suddenly emptied.

Matthias smiled and got to his feet. "Well done, Leonora."

"Thank you, sir." It seemed appropriate.

He took her hand and tucked it into the crook of his elbow. He flipped the summoner open and called for Nathaniel. Leo could see the timer, and it was less than a minute.

"So, what did you learn tonight?"

Daniel and Salleth waved them off as they walked into the growing light.

"I learned that the places the vampires bite as they are made are many and various. They are also worn with pride, or, at least, they blatantly display them."

"Very good."

Nathaniel pulled up, and when the door was open, Leo slid into the back seat.

When Matthias settled in next to her, he asked, "What do you think those marks mean?"

"Mean?"

"Of course. Each location has a meaning. It shows the capacity that the vampire was created for."

He took her hand and stroked her wrist. "A bite on the wrist is rare. It is for administrative capacity." He trailed his fingers up to her bicep. "Here is for a guard or warrior. This is a common mark."

His cool fingers caressed her throat. "This is the most shameful of changes. This indicates that the new vampire was originally a food source. And a mark over the heart is a lover transformed."

"Interesting and more complicated than I imagined. Are there ever bites in the back?"

"No, the topography makes a proper bite difficult. You want something over a vein that will allow for appropriate drainage."

His fingers were still at her neck.

"I will bear that in mind."

"Now, I had to fend off a few offers for you or, at least, a taste of you. Will you consent to wear my mark the next time we go out?"

She blinked. "What would that entail, and is it permanent?"

"It could be reversed with a bit of effort, I mean, if you should ever leave my service." He made it sound unlikely.

"The moment that my kin are safe and I have paid my debt to you, I will seek other employment."

Matthias smiled. "In that case, there is one mark that must be renewed every year that should do just fine."

"Is it painful?"

He shrugged. "That depends on you."

Leo scowled. "How long would it take?"

"You would have to put two hours around midnight in the schedule. Feel free to move things around. It isn't something I can do during daylight."

From her vantage point, she could see Nathaniel's eyes widen in shock.

Matthias spoke clearly. "I trust that you will be circumspect about what you have heard, Nathaniel."

"As always, sir."

Leo asked, "Why is this such a big deal?"

"I am effectively making you my apprentice. It will leave no marks that can be seen by others, but your aura will change. Other blood drinkers and predators will know that you are in my service."

"Is Nathaniel marked like that?"

The car wobbled as the driver snorted.

Matthias chuckled. "No. He does not need it. He isn't human. None of those in my employ are human, with you being the notable exception. I had not counted on what that would mean until tonight. If I am to send you to represent me, you need that protection."

There wasn't much she could say to that. The contract she had signed accounted for reasonable alterations to her physiology in order to ensure she could fulfill her duties.

She took out her phone and checked his schedule. "You have an opening in two days."

"Good. Put your name in. If you are planning on visiting the shifters that I can't work into my schedule, you need to be a little more than human."

Leo didn't know what that entailed, but at least, it was more than human and not less than. She liked being human. In Redbird City, being human made her special. Only fifty percent of the population were visibly human and out of that, only five percent was actually plain, old human.

She watched the flashes of the rising sun as it struggled through the heavy tinting on the windows.

Her thoughts turned to Minny and the baby. She wondered if she could sneak out to visit them. There might be room in the schedule if she got everything updated.

"When we get back to the manor, go for a visit. Have breakfast with your sister. Be back by noon."

She blinked. "Really?"

"Really. Are the updates to the schedule on my computer?"

"They are. The shared file has been updated."

Excitement flared in her. She wasn't going to have to sneak away after all.

She knocked at the door and waited until Minny came up to open it wearing nothing but a nightshirt and fuzzy socks.

"Leo, oh, thank god."

Leo hugged her sister and whispered, "I will take her. You go take a shower. Breakfast will be ready when you are dressed."

"You know I love you."

"I know. Now, go."

Leo found a clean blanket and draped it over

her shoulder. She walked into Minny's bedroom and saw the bright blue eyes of her niece staring up at her from the pink face.

"Hello, Melody. I am your Aunty Leo. I know it is weird, but I will be coming in and out of your life in the next few years." Leo scooped her up and took her to the changing table, clearing her diaper and putting on a clean onesie.

Once the wee one was clean and dressed, Leo went to prepare her famous one-armed breakfast. She perfected it when she was a teen with a broken arm.

Of course, a broken arm didn't squirm, but she still managed an omelette and toast without too much spillage.

Minny looked relieved and refreshed when she emerged from her bedroom. The fluffy slippers screamed comfort.

"Have a seat, Minny."

Leo rocked the baby slightly, and Minny looked at her, the food and the baby and then burst into tears. "I can't do this without you. I need you here."

Leo walked over and stroked her sister's damp hair. "I am here. I just am not at your beck and call twenty-four seven. Have you heard anything at night?"

Minny nodded. "There was snarling and growling last night. Melody didn't like it, but then, there was a sound like a windstorm and everything went quiet, including her."

"Eat your breakfast. We will sort this out."

Minny bent her head and attacked the food on the plate with ravenous energy.

After the breakfast was underway, Leo made one-armed coffee. Melody seemed content to doze on her shoulder.

A knock at the door got her attention. She handed Melody to Minny and dropped the blanket, walking to the door to answer it.

A young blonde woman with perky and pointed ears was smiling at her. "Hello, you must be Miss Leonora."

"Um, yes."

"I am Leela Arguth. Mayor Matthias sent me. He said that you were looking for a nanny for your niece."

Nathaniel was standing in the driveway and giving a thumbs-up, so Leo let her in.

"Oh, of course. Come in. The final decision will be my sister's, but at this point, she would probably accept an ogre as a nanny if she could get a shower."

"Oh, I am no ogre. I am a half-fey half-human with training in early development of magical skills." She smiled brightly again.

Minny called out. "She is hired."

Leo snorted. "Come in and have a seat. Would you like some coffee?"

"Please. I finished my last assignment a month ago, so when the mayor called, I was ready to start immediately. He asked that I wait until this morning."

Leo scowled and went to get coffee. Leela took a seat.

"Miss Arguth, when did the mayor call you?"

"Three days ago. He mentioned that there was

an at-risk baby being hunted and that is just the kind of thing I am very good at."

"Three days ago? Huh." Leo mentally saluted Matthias. "Cream or sugar?"

"Both please."

Leo assembled a tray with coffee for all and brought it to the table.

"Are vampires precognitive as far as you know?" Leo gave Leela a smile.

"No. Their purview is the past, not the future. Why?"

"Because he knew I was looking for a nanny before I did. I wonder how much time this is going to cost me. I am pretty sure that I am going to be in a walker before I pay this off."

She thought about the evening's events and how close she had come to being a snack and mentally added, *If I live that long.*

Chapter Eight

Leo felt like a weight had been lifted off her shoulders. Leela would be moving in that afternoon and taking on her duties as Melody's nanny and Minny's companion.

It hurt a little to be replaced, but she couldn't be everywhere in this equation and still do her part. Her part was at the mayor's side. Her presence there was paying for all of it.

Two nights of normal business activities and taking notes during meetings and she felt she was getting along fairly well. That night was the night she was to be bound to Matthias.

He hadn't told her what it would entail, but she had taken a shower just in case. She was supposed to meet him in half an hour. She wasn't sure what sort of wardrobe choice was appropriate for the activity she was going to engage in. She had no idea what was about to happen.

She was towelling her hair and walking into her closet when she paused. "Well, that solves a problem."

A long, pale, lacy gown was hanging from a hook in the ceiling. The layers would cover her skin and hide what needed to be hidden, but if they shifted at all, she would be as good as buck naked.

It didn't look like underwear was an option. Leo paused and dropped her towel, blanking her mind and simply getting dressed without thinking. If she thought too much, she wouldn't go through with this.

She fluffed her curls out and left them to hang. If she was going au natural, she was going to commit.

She put on some white slippers that had mysteriously appeared on her shoe shelf and checked the time. She had five minutes.

There was nowhere on her dress to put her phone, so she left it in her room in the hopes that once whatever this was was done, she could get back to her new routine.

She desperately wanted to fast forward past what was happening next to get back to her new routine. It was the first time since coming to the manor that she felt actual fear.

This was not a moment she could blush her way through. There was no information on being an apprentice to a vampire in any documentation. She had gone to sleep with her laptop on the covers in search of the missing piece of information. It was plugged into the spare charger in her quarters right now.

A quiet knock on the door got her attention. She opened it. Reed was standing there, and a smile crossed his features. "Excellent. Come this way, please."

She left her room and closed the door. There

were no locks on her door, but as this was an obscure part of the manor, no one frequented the area.

Her lace dress fluttered and let any and all air caress her skin as she walked. "Reed, is it you that sneaks into my room at night and messes with my wardrobe?"

"No, Ms. Wicks. That is the province of Dorn."

"That just elevated this to a level of creepy I didn't think it was possible to reach. He doesn't like me."

"He doesn't like strangers. Give him a decade. He will loosen up."

She nodded and tensed up as they left the familiar halls and he led her outside into the gardens behind the manor. Leo held in her gasp. She hadn't realized that it was a night garden, but that made sense.

"This way, please."

Reed led her through the hedge maze lit by a rainbow of glowing flowers.

Matthias was sitting next to a fountain in the centre, reading by the light of the glowing roses.

Reed left the same way they had come—without a word.

Leo stepped forward until she was next to Matthias, and she waited.

He patted the stone bench beside him without looking up.

Leo took the seat and winced at the cool surface under her skin. The heat from the day had long since dissipated.

"Before there were vampires, there was the

wave. It brought magic to the world but not all of that magic was used for good. I lived in a small city with my parents and other family, including my brother. Our city was at war with a neighbour. The king of the next city cursed us with a plague that swept through the children and elderly first, taking our parents with it."

He turned a page in the book. "We had been told that the tree of life could save the rest of our people. My brother and I were still alive and reasonably healthy, so we went in search of the tree."

The picture in the book was an old, gnarled tree with fruit in the low-slung branches.

"We walked for days and nights, sleeping only when we had to and eating what we could find. We were near death when we finally found it. It appeared in front of us, and my brother pushed me to the side, running for the tree. Instead of gathering the fruit, he used his knife to slash at the trunk and stab at the tree, drinking in its sap. Night was coming, and he grew strong as he took what he wanted."

He laughed slightly. "I ran up and tried to stop him. He batted me aside then smashed me into the tree itself. I felt myself dying. Life was fading away. I asked him if he would take the fruit to our people. He called me a child and laughed again, the new fangs of the hunter showing in his mad expression."

Leo didn't say a word. She listened.

"I felt myself leaving my body, but then, a cool touch on my lips woke me, brought me back. A bough from the tree was bent, and instead of the red sluggish sap my brother had taken, I was given bright, green life. The tree fed me through the night and into the next morning. When I was strong enough, I asked for the fruit, and the tree gave it, whispering how to use it in my mind."

"I ran home as fast as I could, but as fast as I could move, I could not outrun death. He had already visited and gone."

He sighed. "There was no one to save, so I went out looking for other victims of the demon-witch who had destroyed my family. I found another village near a rich mine, and it was in the early stages of the plague. I fed them from the fruit and healed them. One of the young survivors had lost her parents in the first wave of disease, and she asked to come with me. I felt the whisper in my mind of what I needed to do, and I made my first vampire. I gave her purpose, and she followed me."

"A century later, my followers and I met the followers of my brother, and we stopped their rampage of gore and abuse. It was the first fight between us. He had created hundreds of those just like him. We sought them out, looking for the source, until the day came that I faced my brother, and I did what I had to."

She wanted to ask, but she kept quiet.

"I gave him an eternity of silence. I retrieved what he had taken from the tree and returned it to the earth. I became the ruler of his followers and my own, but there was never peace between us. They are driven to kill; we are not."

He flipped the pages again. "In my lifetime, I have spoken with the tree at length. I asked it why

I had to be alone."

Leo was confused; he said he had followers.

"The tree told me that I had to find someone who valued life above anything, to make them my apprentice and teach them my ways. When they made the choice to join me permanently, it would be joyous and I would no longer be alone."

She had to ask. "How many apprentices have you had?"

"Twenty-three. Each seemed a good choice when we began, but as time went on, we drew further and further apart until they sought out someone else."

"Where are they now?"

"Most have surrendered to eternity after long and happy lives."

She blinked. "They were human?"

"Until the day they died. This will not change what you are, but it will provide a layer of protection that you currently do not have."

He looked at her, and his gaze drifted southward and then up again. "The dress isn't strictly necessary, but I do enjoy it."

She blushed. "Dorn brought it."

"Dorn will have you dressed like a hooker if you let him."

She laughed at the frank statement. "What comes next?"

"I mark you. It won't be anywhere that can be misconstrued as a maker's mark, but it will be a definite mark that connects us."

"How long will it last?"

"A year from tonight. If you don't wish to continue under my protection after that, it will fade away." He got to his feet, put the book down and offered her his hand.

A raised stone was around the corner of a glowing hedge.

Leo bit her lip. "If you are looking for a virgin sacrifice, you are a little late."

His laugh rang out and the flowers quivered. "Good to know. In full disclosure, this will stop you from aging for the next year, which means that your moon time will not occur."

She deciphered it and blushed. "Oh. Right. No great loss."

He turned with a sudden move and picked her up, placing her gently on the stone. Her legs were draped over the edge, and when he parted her thighs, she felt herself panicking again. "Where exactly is this mark going?"

"Your inner thigh. It should not hurt." He stroked her dress up and carefully arranged the lace so that she was still completely covered.

It made her feel more exposed than just lying there naked would have, but she held still when his cool hands smoothed her skin, holding the lace down.

She didn't feel his breath, but his tongue flicked out. Leo jumped a little. He held her thigh and pressed his teeth into her with the lightest pressure.

The word *femoral artery* ran through her mind as the teeth sank deeper. The sudden suction on her inner thigh sent pulses of arousal through her. Leo flailed around and gripped the edges of the stone, and she arched and hissed as he continued to drink.

This was more than marking.

Her self-control was wearing thin, and the moment he shifted his hand to cover her sex, it broke. She jerked and shivered, gasping as her body tried to clench down on an invader that wasn't inside her.

She was sweating lightly and completely limp when Matthias licked the small wounds closed. He lifted his head and licked his lips. "That was new."

Her blush could have started a fire. "I..." She couldn't finish it. Aside from a slight lightheaded feeling, there was something new inside her.

"I must say, that was definitely a stirring reaction." He eased her dress back over her thighs and moved to help her sit up.

It took some effort to unclench her hands from the stone, but he managed to get her to a sitting position. She was mortified.

"I am sorry that I... you know."

"Came? Do not apologize. It is the first time I have caused that reaction while tagging an apprentice. You held back, so well done."

"How do you know that?"

"Leonora, I have known you for a week, and you always hold back." He smiled and pressed a kiss to her temple.

"I guess it is back to work then."

He laughed. "First, we will go to the dining room and you will have a large meal. I didn't intend to, but I drank quite a bit. I got a little carried away. The link has been forged, so while we got distracted, we managed to get the job done."

She froze when he picked her up again.

"What are you doing?"

"I am carrying you in to the dining room. Trust me, you are in no shape to walk, and our connection won't kick in until sunrise."

"Oh, I guess that was in the fine print." She tried to stay flippant, but it was difficult when all she wanted to do was lean against his shoulder and enjoy the ride.

He held her carefully as if afraid she would break. She was happy that they didn't meet up with Reed. Her current position put her at a disadvantage.

The dining room was empty except for some covered dishes at one end. Matthias walked right to the chair, and instead of setting her down, he settled into it himself.

"Please, eat."

She slowly turned in his lap and accepted him as her personal chair. Leo wasn't one to ignore her stomach, so she uncovered the plates and grabbed a fork.

Being a human sacrifice was hungry work.

Chapter Nine

When she tasted a food that she really enjoyed, she felt a shiver run through Matthias. After her immediate hunger was satisfied, she turned and stared into his eyes.

"The link works both ways?"

He was sitting with his eyes closed and a blissful expression on his cool features. "Yes, it does. You have an exceptionally sensitive sense of taste. It dissects everything and enjoys the components."

She shrugged. "It has always been that way. It makes it easier to reproduce the food I like."

She tried to ease herself off his lap, but his hands gripped her hips and his eyes opened. "Where are you going?"

"I was going to my room to get changed and get to work."

He sighed. "You have not eaten enough, and you definitely did not drink enough."

She grumbled and pivoted back toward the table, filling her glass with water before chugging it down. The burp when she finished was inevitable. Leo glared at him. "Better?"

"A start. Reed will bring you a tray." He let her go.

She wobbled a bit when she stood, but she didn't want him to carry her again. With tremendous effort, she left the dining room and headed for her chambers.

Reed saw her and smiled brightly. "Come this way, Ms. Wicks. Your quarters have been moved closer to the mayor's."

She was a little foggy. "Why?"

"You are his apprentice now. Your proximity will help if you or he require anything during quiet hours." Reed smiled happily. "There have not been any apprentices in the last five decades, so the staff is very excited."

She swayed. "Excited?"

"It means that the mayor will be in a much better mood. That is a win-win situation for all of the staff."

He turned to lead her to the new quarters, but he was fading into a tunnel as her vision blurred. Hands caught her, and Matthias lifted her again.

She looked up at him and muttered, "Dammit," before she fainted.

Matthias looked down at the woman in his arms, and he sighed. "She is stubborn."

Reed inclined his head. "I believe that is why you chose her, sir."

Matthias chuckled. "I believe you are right. She has a devotion to family that I found admirable and a self-possession that is truly amazing."

"She is definitely a force to be reckoned with,

sir. I have put her in the silver room."

"Good." Matthias moved with speed and settled her in her bed before going into her closet and selecting a dress, underwear and shoes for her. He kept the heels low because she was going to be unstable until she got some proper rest and her body embraced the small bit of the tree that he had pressed into her bloodstream.

"Where am I?"

He sat next to her and waited for her to sit up. "You are in your new rooms. We have a bit of work to finish tonight, so if you could get dressed and meet me in the office, I would appreciate it."

He gave her a small kiss on her pursed lips, and her eyes widened in surprise.

He was still grinning twenty minutes later when she entered the office with her laptop and her phone in tow.

She settled at her desk and flicked him a quick glance. He watched the colour rise in her cheeks.

Matthias had tasted women for the last few thousand years and none had struck him with the clear purity of soul that Leonora had exhibited. She spent most of her time holding back her passion, her enthusiasm and her enjoyment of the world around her. She felt it; she just hid it.

Matthias was going to enjoy the link between himself and this woman who spent more time holding herself back than she did living her life. He was going to see what he could do to shift that balance.

Leo glanced up and blushed. Matthias was staring

at her with a smirk on his lips. It was a calculated look that appeared to be analyzing her.

"Yes, Mr. Mayor? Was there something you needed?"

He inclined his head. "I would like to go over your schedule with you. I have gotten some correspondence that requires action, but I am unable to go myself. Come here and I will explain what needs to be done."

He got up from his desk and took a seat on one of the couches near the fireplace.

She grabbed her phone and left her desk to sit a polite distance from him.

He held up some of the heavy linen paper, similar to what he used for his own personal correspondence. "I have received a request for a mediator."

"All right. What is that?"

He smiled and laid out the situation. A dragon's wife—the vampire healer Zora—wished to buy a friend's freedom from the vampire king Olvadi. The problem arose in that Octavia—the vampire in question—was one of Olvadi's favourites.

"What do I have to do?"

"Represent me and keep both parties calm. Regick will have his lawyers speaking for him, but Olvadi likes the attack and retreat of negotiations. It is what makes him feel alive."

"So, he is a taken vampire."

"He is. I have heard that Zora's healing has managed to regenerate him to some extent, and he is using that new energy to inflict himself on anything that crosses his path. He will take you if you don't defend yourself."

Leo was more than a little nervous at that. "Why send me at all?"

"Because Regick is a strong ally and a good friend. If he has asked me for help, I will offer it. Do not worry. I am sending you with my most trusted guards." He reached out and touched her hand.

Her burgeoning panic eased, and she breathed evenly. "All right. When do I go?"

"You will need to fly out today at dusk. You will only be gone for two days; if there is anything additionally needed, I will send someone to replace you."

She swallowed. "Today? Wow. That is quick."

"I know. I have been putting this off as long as I could, but now that you are my apprentice, you are in the perfect position to take over some of my distant representation."

"Why?"

He squeezed her hand again. "Vampires are territorial and I have killed far too many of them in my life. If my presence can be accepted without my being there, it is a step forward."

"And it expands your control."

Matthias shrugged slightly. "That as well."

She sighed. "Right. Well, can I get some rest before I go?"

He nodded. "Of course. The helicopter will pick you up in front of the manor at seven this evening."

She nodded. "Right, so where am I going?"

"The shadow city of Arbor. Daysiders and nightsiders split the population, but Olvadi rules them all. Regick owns most of the city. He has the resources to barter with, but he is not in the correct position to strike a deal."

"Because of his wife."

"Because he and Olvadi have a truce. If Olvadi gives in, he loses face; if Regick insists, he starts a war."

"That would be bad."

"Indeed. You have the rest of today to learn what you can about the parties involved, and then, you must get some rest. At midnight tonight, the link between us will be sealed."

"And I will be in another city." It made her feel nervous. Sealing seemed like something that would be visible.

He shrugged. "It can't be helped."

"Right. Well, in that case, I should go over the donations to the museum before I crash for a while. The director is probably rushing the morning couriers daily."

"You are right. This way." He rose and tugged at her hand, pulling her to her feet.

She walked with him. He tucked her hand in the crook of his elbow with a gesture so natural that she knew he had done it hundreds of times.

They headed toward her new room, and he led her past it to the door at the end of the hall. He opened the door, and they were in a room that made her apartments look teeny.

"These are my quarters. Feel free to visit if you need to talk."

Somehow, when he said the word *talk,* it sounded far more intriguing than it should. He walked past the fireplace and pressed his hand to the wall. Hard. A stone shifted and a doorway opened.

"Keep hold of my hand. There are objects down here that do not enjoy daylight, but red lamps are inside the display room."

She took his hand and followed him down a set of steep stairs into the darkness.

At the bottom of the steps, he put an arm around her and pulled her into a small vestibule. While she was plastered against him, he reached behind her and opened another door. He steered her through it and closed the door behind them until they were in absolute darkness.

Leo could hear her breathing and nothing else.

"I am turning the red light on."

She heard the soft click of a switch, and red light bathed a warehouse full of items on display.

"Oh my..." She looked at the books, scrolls, daggers, tablets and thousands of other items in the collection.

"Choose what you think the director would get the most use out of. The blood chalice of Irka-Set is particularly charming." He walked over to a cup carved out of ruby.

"Why would you part with any of this?" She looked around and waved her hands at the displays.

"To have you at my side, of course. It is a price I was more than willing to pay, and I still am."

She was glad the red light would hide the blush that he seemed to bring on so easily. "Well, show me what you had in mind when it came up. You must have had some items in mind. Oh, but they do need to be light safe."

"Right. Well, this is the blood chalice used by an ancient god to turn his people from mortal into immortal. It would be a good choice and an excellent draw."

"It seems priceless."

He chuckled and drew her down the line. "Everything in this room is. They are parts of vampire history. Having them on public display would be good for our social profile."

He showed her nineteen items that he was considering for display.

"Too many. Keep it to ten and add to the collection every year as a tax deduction. You get to have them pay for the security to store it and insure it, and there is more room to keep your collection growing. Do you have provenance for all of this?"

"In the podium under the item. Each one has a full binder of all origin documentation." Matthias smiled. "Have I mentioned how I enjoy your changing modes from embarrassed to workplace Valkyrie looking for victims?"

She felt the embarrassment rush over her again. "Um, it isn't something I really have control over."

He pulled her toward him, and he leaned down to kiss her softly. "Pick your ten and I will have them sent over to the museum."

She rattled off her list, and he smiled; the expression was eerie in the light.

He took her hand and led her back to the entrance, turning off the light before opening the door. She stumbled when they climbed the stairs, and he caught her, holding her to his side as they walked up into the daylight world.

He escorted her back to her room. "Go to sleep. Your purse, laptop and meal have all been delivered."

"How do you do that?"

Matthias laughed and held up his phone. "I can text and talk at the same time. The modern age is truly a marvel. Reed loves his phone."

"What about Dorn?"

"Well, he is slow to change."

Leo snickered. "Well, if I don't see you before I leave, have a nice weekend."

"Oh, you will see me. As I am sending you into the lair of a vampire king, you will bring a gift from me. It might not be enjoyable to deliver it, but you are my assistant."

With that cryptic mention, he walked away. She decided not to worry about what she had to bring.

As Leo stepped into her bedroom and closed the door behind her, she sent a text to her sister. *Tonight, I get to ride in a helicopter! Wheeee!*

Chapter Ten

Matthias slid his hand under her hair and kissed her wildly. Leo froze in shock for a moment until her heart started pounding and her palms found themselves pressed against his chest. When he let her go, she looked at her guards, and they both had politely disinterested looks on their faces.

"I am supposed to give *that* to Olvadi?" She licked her lips, and his eyes lit as he watched the movement.

"Oh, no. I have a lily watered with my own blood." He waved his hand, and Dorn walked up to them with the lily in his hands.

She frowned. "Then what was the kiss?"

"Practice. I will see you when you get back, Leonora."

She took the lily and walked to the helicopter that was sitting in the centre of the huge lawn.

Leo sat between Lima and Coren. She was a dwarf and he was a pixie. They both looked like they ate horseshoes for breakfast.

She put on the protective headphones and sat back as the blades of the helicopter began to whirl. She dug her phone out of the purse that Coren was watching over, and as they lifted off, she took pictures of the manor, the city and the skyline.

When she had finished being a tourist, she put her phone away and sat there, rubbing her fingers over her lips for the rest of the one-hour trip.

The city of Arbor was lovely, and the skyscrapers were attention getting. Redbird seemed small in comparison.

"Where are we going to land?"

Coren grinned. "On the tower of the dragon of Arbor."

The tower in question was a mirrored-glass building that spiked the sky. The helicopter lined up, and the pilot landed them efficiently.

Two figures were waiting for them on the helipad.

Lima got out and held out her hand. Leo took the hint and exited the aircraft. Coren carried her bag and her computer.

A woman with long black hair came forward with a smile. "Hello. You must be Ms. Wicks."

"I am; you can call me Leo."

"I am Zora; this is Regick. We will be your hosts for the next two days."

Leo shook Zora's hand and then turned to the man with golden skin next to her. "Pleased to meet you."

He looked her over, and his lips quirked in a smile. "Matthias has surprised me again."

He extended his hand, and she took it. The power that he exuded was palpable; it went along with the easy attitude of control.

She brushed off the comment and smiled.

"These are my… companions. Lima and Coren."

Zora nodded; a gust of wind whipped her hair around Regick. Surprisingly, he smiled.

Leo blanked her face. "Please, lead the way."

She wasn't going to involve herself in their lives, as curious as she was about their relationship. She had never met a dragon shifter before. The final briefing that she had gotten in the yard before she left had told her one thing—mind her own business. Some species didn't enjoy questions.

She followed her hosts, and her guards followed her. They were basically with her to make sure that she ate regularly and was not molested in a permanent fashion. Apparently, temporary molestation was fine.

They headed down to a living level—a penthouse that was completely astonishing in the views that it afforded of the skyline.

A gargoyle was waiting next to a stack of documents at a wide table, and when she sat down with the dragon, his wife and the gargoyle, she found out what they were willing to pay for the freedom of Octavia.

When she had all of the information, she finished the cup of tea and checked the clock. It was only ten in the evening. She was probably going to faint when the connection to Matthias kicked in and that was going to hurt her position as his representative.

She had two hours to complete this entire process, or at least to introduce herself and start the negotiations.

She tapped the lily and smiled at the scent that

shivered out of the flower.

Zora looked from Leo to the gargoyle. "Are you ready?"

Leo nodded. "I am ready. We can leave whenever Leah is ready."

The gargoyle nodded and smiled. "I am ready. Let's bring Octavia home."

Leo got to her feet, picked up her plant and followed the gargoyle out of the building and into an SUV limo. Lima and Coren were with her all the way.

She hadn't anticipated being kept waiting. The clock ticked by, and it was eleven by the time she was able to introduce herself to the vampire king.

"Greetings, your majesty, from Matthias of Redbird City. I have brought you a gift from Matthias." She nodded her head and then met his crimson gaze.

Olvadi leaned forward and laughed. "He sends me a flower? I thought that you were the gift."

She inclined her head. "I have in my hands a lily watered with Matthias's own blood."

The laughter died. "You are serious?"

"Delivered to me the moment before I left."

Olvadi nodded to one of his attendants, and the skittish vampire nearly dropped the lily as she carried it over to her king.

The king took it with reverence, inhaling the fragrance. "It is a princely gift. I will have to offer him something of equal value."

"I believe you are aware of the reason that I am here."

He sighed and made a gesture.

A pale, thin vampire called out, "Court is closed."

Olvadi heaved himself to his feet, and he towered over her. He reached out and touched Leo's cheek. "Matthias has surprised me."

"Apparently, he does that a lot."

He turned and left the room. She followed him with her entourage trailing after. Leah, Coren and Lima stayed close. They walked up some long, low stairs, down some hallways and into a boardroom.

The woman with the shaking hands was at his side, flinching whenever he moved. He sprawled lazily in his chair—the literal king of all he surveyed.

Leah faced him across the table, seated with her wings folded behind her, and Leonora stood next to the table, between them as arbitrator.

"We are here to obtain the possession of the vampire Octavia."

Olvadi reached out and pulled Octavia against his side. "I do not think so. She has been mine for centuries, and I will not release her any time soon."

Leonora watched as Octavia's emotional stability cracked, just for an instant.

This was why she was here. "Your majesty, as you are aware, if a fair offer is made for one of your retainers, you must at least listen to it."

He looked at her and gave her a slow leer from head to toe. In a moment, he was out of his chair and had grabbed her to pin her against the wall. He slid his hand up her inner thigh. "What will Matthias give me to consider it?"

When his rough fingers caressed the marks that Matthias had left on her, she felt a surge of heat that filled her from her core outward. She grabbed Olvadi's throat and squeezed. The sensation must have startled him, because he dropped his hand and stepped back.

"I am here to ensure that you listen to the offer, Olvadi. I gave you all the respect due you as king of this city, but you will not lay hands on the apprentice of Matthias again."

Olvadi's eyes widened as she backed him up to his chair.

"Resume negotiations and resign yourself that Octavia will be leaving your service."

He scowled. "I do not wish to part with her."

"You assaulted a representative of Matthias. Be happy that this is all he demands." Leo stood silently and watched as the threat she had issued was obeyed. *Cool.*

Her body was humming with energy, and her mind was calm. A green wash had come over her senses, and she could see the seething red of Olvadi, the cool pearl colour of Leah and the rioting hot pink of Octavia.

Lima and Coren were a shade of pale green, one swirling with grey and one with blue.

She glanced down at herself, and she was bright emerald green, swirling with a soft violet. *Huh. Neat.*

The connection between her and Matthias hadn't been too bad after all. It had come a little early. She was going to have to look into that.

She remained on her feet for hours. Checking

the two negotiators when they slipped up and got personal was a little strange, but it wasn't the first time she had seen a negotiation. It was, however, the first time that she had seen a negotiation for a living being.

The territories and buildings that were being offered were impressive, but Olvadi pressed for more. Octavia was being offered for far more than market value.

She was hungry, tired, and she had had enough. Leo slammed her hand down on the table. "Enough."

It amused her that even Olvadi jumped.

Leo turned. "Olvadi, you are a king, the ruler of a city that has laws guarding the rights of nightsiders and daysiders?"

"Correct."

"And yet, you reserve the right to torture one of your own people for no crime or offense committed. How is it that you are above your own laws?"

"I am the king."

She cocked her head. "So, by that logic, I could take your head off and rule over your people simply because I can?"

"It would mean war." He jutted his chin out, but she could see indecision flickering in his eyes.

Leo tsked. "Not really. A city under my rule would be a fair and just place with the offenders punished."

"You could not."

Leo pointed at Olvadi, and he lifted from his chair to be pinned on the ceiling. She felt him scrabbling at her mind, and she smiled as he ran up against the wall of her calm.

"You will agree to the sale price of the two nightclubs, the ninety acres of land outside the city and the tailor shops."

He thrashed, but she held him to the ceiling. "Agreed."

"None of those here will speak of the means by which the negotiations concluded." She lowered him back into his seat.

He cocked his head. "What do you mean I was torturing her?"

"She prefers women. Your attentions were unwanted and unwelcome. That is a type of torture that you should be aware of."

He blinked. "What do you mean?"

"I have read your dossier. Matthias provided me with all the information I would need to understand your motivations. You have had a rough existence, but it is up to you to wish more for your followers and offspring."

He looked confused. "Fine. Take her."

Octavia looked shocked and stepped forward, but Leo held up her hand. "Not quite yet. Leah, draw it up."

The signing of the sale was the first part.

"Olvadi, as you have signed, you must now free her."

He muttered, "I free you."

Octavia smiled faintly. "Thank you."

Leo stopped Leah and Octavia from leaving. "Not quite yet. Olvadi, give Octavia your blood."

He jolted. "How do you know that?"

She sighed. "I am Matthias's apprentice. Just

do it and complete freeing her."

Octavia looked uncertain, but when Olvadi bit his finger and extended his hand to her, she bowed over his hand and licked the dark-crimson drop.

An electrified expression took Octavia over, and she fainted.

Olvadi scowled. "I trust you will come for a visit before you leave tomorrow."

"Of course. Now that business is concluded, the social aspect of my visit can commence." She smiled and inclined her head.

"Excellent. I am throwing a party in your honour, and I hope your wardrobe is up to it." He smiled tightly.

She nodded to Leah and turned to Lima. "Please carry Octavia. She is going to need some care before she settles into the peculiar situation she is now in."

The dwarf lifted the unconscious vampire in her arms and carried her out through the halls. Leah followed, Leonora was behind her and Coren protected her back.

Their party was through the door and on the way to Regick's home in ten minutes. It was the longest walk of her life.

Fifty hungry vampires trying to stare through her skin was enough to unnerve anyone, but she kept her aspect calm and cold. It took all her powers of concentration, but she made it to the vehicle. There would be time to break down later.

chapter eleven

Leo went straight to the quarters put aside for her, and she went to bed. She was going to need all of her strength for the evening ahead.

Octavia was still unconscious and going to remain so for a day or two. That was what Matthias's text had told Leo when she had asked him in the vehicle.

He had also told her not to worry about what Olvadi had in store. No harm would come to her.

His words had done wonders to soothe her.

She crawled into the king-sized bed, and she went to sleep. It wasn't even weird to sleep as dawn struck. She was getting used to it.

Zora had to know. "How did she get him to agree?"

Leah opened her mouth, but nothing came out. "I don't think I can say."

"Were you sworn to secrecy?"

"No. I just don't think I can say. The words won't come out. I can say that she didn't do anything untoward. The agreement was come to using law and tradition." Leah exhaled in relief.

Zora chuckled. "Well, as long as that is what happened and Octavia remains free, I am good with it."

"Leonora's vampire said that Octavia would sleep for a few days. She will come to and have her freedom."

Regick wrapped his arms around Zora. She leaned back against him. "Can we trust Matthias?"

He kissed her temple. "We can. If he says she is free, she is free. Where did Leonora go?"

Leah smiled. "She was tired. She is resting. She still has to attend Olvadi's official welcome ceremony. She muttered something about needing her strength."

Zora felt queasy. "She has to go back there?"

"She does. She said that was the scariest part of the whole visit." Leah shrugged.

Zora understood. Olvadi's taste in parties tended to be on the bacchanalia side of things. From what she had witnessed, it was not really Leonora's scene.

Leo got up, grabbed a shower and pinned her hair up in a loose bun. She slipped a robe on and went in search of food.

Lima and Coren were sitting in the dining room. Coren's wings were open and sticking out on either side of the chair back. They had a shining metallic edge and looked a little deadlier than something so transparent and delicate should.

"Good... morning?" Leo winced.

Lima grinned and got to her feet. "Good morning. You just caught it. Five minutes from now it would have been good afternoon."

Leo headed for the kitchen, but Lima held her hand up. "Sit. You haven't eaten in quite a while. I will bring something in for you."

Leo snorted and raised her brows. "Does it involve coffee?"

"Of course."

"Excellent. I only get tea at the manor house. It is driving me nuts."

Lima laughed, and Leo turned to join Coren at the table.

Coren was reading a tablet and flicking through yesterday's news. Leo caught a glimpse of the pictures and stared at the images of herself.

"What does that say?"

Coren grinned. "Basically, the moment we left, Matthias held a press conference that announced you as his new assistant and representative, acting ambassador of Redbird City."

Leo sat back and grunted. "Well, hell. I can figure out why he chose now to send me to Arbor."

"Why?"

"Because I would kick his butt if he tried to make me an ambassador and I was close enough to reach him."

Coren gave her a long look, and then, he laughed. "I think you would."

Lima brought her a cup of coffee, and she smirked. "And he would let her."

Leo blinked. "Why would you think that?"

Lima grinned and headed back to the kitchen without saying a word.

The coffee had two creams and two sugars, just the way she liked it.

When Lima reappeared with a plate that contained an omelette and two pieces of toast, Leo asked. "How did you know how I take my coffee?"

Lima hopped up onto her chair again. "I texted your sister. She is a fount of information. Your niece is doing well, by the way. She texted you a few pictures of the baby. They came through on your phone."

"And my phone is..."

"On the charger."

Coren continued to read the news on his tablet.

"Where are we, exactly?"

"Three floors below the penthouse housing Zora and Regick." Coren spoke absently.

"Where is Octavia?"

"She is on the floor above ours."

"I would like to see her after I eat." Leo nibbled at her toast.

Coren glanced at her. "Of course. Would you care to get dressed before we go?"

She shrugged and looked down. "Nope. I am good. Since I have to get fancy for this evening's activities, I prefer to spend the day as comfortable as I can."

"You will want to keep the robe closed then." Coren looked at her and smiled.

"Generally, yes. I would pin it, but I don't have pins." She bit into the omelette but paused. "This tastes like it does at the manor."

Lima smiled. "I am your cook. The mayor would not trust anyone else with your safety."

Leo ate and smiled. "It is still excellent, no matter where we are. I can't believe I slept as long as I did."

"Well, your schedule is ahead an hour because we travelled eastward, so you will be hungrier than the time allows."

Leo paused. "That is why the bonding kicked in so early. Thank goodness. I was wondering about that."

Coren put the tablet aside. "Is that when Olvadi laid hands on you?"

"Yup. I feel fine now though. It seems that the original surge of energy has worn off." Leo finished her breakfast, and she lifted the plate up before Lima could help.

She washed her dishes and put them away once she dried them. The apartment was all set up for visitors.

A knock at the door had Coren in motion. He flipped out of the chair and was over to the peephole in a blur of wings.

He opened the door, smiling at the guest. "Miss Zora. Good afternoon."

"Thank you, Coren. Is she awake?"

Leo stepped forward. "If I am she, then yes, she is."

Zora ran up to her and hugged her. "Thank you so much. Leah can't say how it happened, but she said that you had to take extreme measures."

Leo grunted with the impact, but she smiled. "They weren't that extreme. I just am a little less than enthusiastic about returning there tonight."

Zora released her and wiped tears from her eyes. "I know that wanting her free was a bit of a silly thing, but it means a lot to have her loose."

Lima asked, "Would you care for some coffee? I have a pot on."

Zora smiled. "Please."

Leo nodded as well with a thumbs-up. "Come on and tell me about her."

They sat together in the living room, sipping coffee and talking about Octavia.

"When do you think she will wake up, and how hungry will she be?" Zora finally asked the questions that had obviously been on her mind.

"Oh, she will sleep for a few days, and she won't be hungry for blood. Like other given vampires, she will be able to consume energy from those around her. She will need to be in a crowd at least once a week."

"She is a taken vampire. She was made centuries ago." Zora looked confused.

"That is where it gets a little odd. I am only telling you this because you won't remember the details. No one does. So, Olvadi gave her his blood after he freed her. It undid the bond between them, which left her with a transformed body and no master. Her system is setting itself to not needing blood right now. When she wakes, she will be able to drink it if she chooses, but she won't need it to survive."

"Why won't I remember the details?" Zora looked amused.

Leo shrugged. "I don't know. I just know you

won't."

How Matthias's blood worked in this situation had trickled into her mind along with the power rush. It wasn't as sharp as it had been, but she knew that the information wouldn't last. It was not for the taken to know how the given worked.

"Would you care to hit the spa this afternoon? The building is pretty fully stocked with businesses."

Leo wrinkled her nose. "If you don't mind, I would rather just catch up on my emails so that there won't be as much backlog when I get home. I am here on business after all."

"Fair enough. I just want you to know that your efforts are appreciated." Zora smiled. "Call if you need anything, and I will see you before you leave."

"You will?"

Zora got to her feet and laughed. "This is the only building the helicopter can land on. I will be seeing you again."

Just like that, her hostess was gone and Leo was free to pursue her love of order by attending to the emails in her account that needed answering. Images of Melody were in every three emails, and it helped the day whiz by.

When the sun was setting, Coren entered her room, closed her computer and pulled out a garment bag. "Go and eat. Lima has a burger and fries for you."

"What are you doing?"

"When you are done, I am going to lace you into this, so keep that in mind." Coren smiled.

"Well, that is a tempting offer, but I think that

Lima can help me."

"She can't reach." Coren winked. "Go eat. Your food is getting cold."

Leo got up, tightened her robe and stalked into the dining room. The moment she cleared the bedroom door, she grinned and it remained on her face until she finished the delectable burger, ran her fries through the drippings and got up to get dressed. Suddenly, she had the premonition that this was going to be the hardest part of the night.

"Don't you dare." Leo scowled at Coren, but he grinned and took a picture of her with his phone.

"I am sorry, Ms. Wicks. I had to. Matthias's instructions. Olvadi could not be the first vampire king to see you in this."

The vest was skin tight and embossed leather. Her skirt was laced from mid-thigh to hip. The shoes that she was wearing were held in place by the thinnest straps she could imagine and wrapped up to her calf. Coren hadn't been kidding. The lacing was involved and the four-foot dwarf would have had a problem with getting the upper lacing on her bodice.

Coren also had skills with hairstyling. Her hair had been pulled up into a tumbling wave that went down her back.

There was no way that anyone would mistake her for a vampire. All the places where vampires bit their children were exposed and unblemished.

Once the picture was taken, Coren wrapped her in a cloak embossed with golden branches and crimson fruit.

It was after eight in the evening, and Leo gave herself a final look in the mirror before she left with her guards. Her bags were packed for the return trip, and Regick's people would bring them up to the helipad when they were on their way back.

For now, she had her phone and her guards. That would have to be enough for the evening. She didn't have anything else to hide behind.

Chapter Twelve

The court had a different vibe when she arrived. There was an excited tension that she hadn't anticipated. They knew something she didn't know, and Matthias hadn't told her what it was.

"Ambassador, thank you for gracing us with your presence." Olvadi's major-domo bowed and offered to take her cloak.

Coren raised his hand and stepped around, making the vampire jump back to avoid the razor wings. He gave her a solemn look before he unfasteded her cloak and removed it with a flourish. He folded it over his arm and stepped aside.

She whispered, "Stay close; you have my phone."

He winked and stepped behind her again, leaving her to face the lounging Olvadi.

Leo inclined her head slightly and stood straight once again. "Good evening, your majesty."

"I hear that I am being graced by Ambassador Wicks." He quirked his lips while he looked her over.

"Apparently Mayor Matthias has decided to elevate me to the status of representative while I have been away from the office." She gave him a bland look. "I must thank him properly when I return home."

Olvadi raised his brows. "You are not pleased with your status?"

"I do not truly enjoy surprises." She didn't add that her normal response to surprises was violence. He didn't need to know that.

He got to his feet and walked toward her. He extended his hand to her, and protocol meant she had to put her hand in his.

The cool touch of his fingers was distasteful. Still, he closed his fingers over hers and pulled her hand to his lips. When his tongue flicked out to taste her skin, it was a touch so light she should not have felt it, but she did.

"I have events planned for your entertainment, Ambassador. Come this way."

He kept hold of her hand and walked her through the crowd and into a wide ballroom that had a dais at one end and a whole lot of cushions stacked against the walls. This boded ill.

He settled her in one of the seats, and she could feel the velvet rubbing against her thigh through the slit and laces.

Olvadi took the seat next to her, and he clapped. "Now, Ambassador, I know that you have only been amongst our people for a bit over a week, which means you are unaware of our ways. I thought to help Matthias with your training by demonstrating some of the perks of the vampire life."

It sounded ominous, so she held in her emotional response as music started and gyrating dancers took the floor.

Leo watched the naked men and women move rhythmically and predictably into energetic sex in a staggering variety of positions.

Despite the display, she felt cold. This was designed to shock or arouse her, and she would give Olvadi neither reaction.

When the music faded, Leo applauded politely. "Very nicely done."

The dancers bowed and looked to Olvadi. He glared at Leo and then clapped for the next group of dancers.

Blood and fire was the theme for this dance. Blades were used to cut themselves until the coppery scent thickened the air. Torches were brought in, and the dancers burned each other in ritual fashion. The smell of burned flesh wasn't pleasant. Leo blinked at the acrid scent and continued to watch the highly choreographed performance.

It could have been worse, but there was no screaming. The dancers performed as blandly as Leo felt.

It was a relief when the dance was done.

Olvadi got to his feet, and he came around to stare at her. "You aren't enjoying this?"

"I am. It is lovely to watch. I am very impressed at the limber motions of the vampires as a people."

"Perhaps this will gain your favour."

Behind him, she could see a dozen people scrubbing the floors to remove the blood and ash.

"My favour doesn't matter. It is Matthias's good will that you gain by my entertainment."

"I do not wish to impress another vampire

king. I want to impress you. You are pure and untouched and yet have an ancient soul. It is a perplexing mix. What does it take to make your blood rise?"

The cleaners scuttled away, and he backed onto the floor, clapping his hands one final time.

Women in clothing so minimal it was hardly even there mixed with men wearing tiny pouches over their groins. They walked to Olvadi and ran their hands over him, stripping him down with methodical care.

Olvadi remained on his feet and watched her the whole time as one of the women sucked his cock, another man and woman bit at his nipples and the rest of them sucked and licked at whatever body part was free.

It seemed that the final entertainment was an Olvadi-central orgy. She sat back and watched.

At a silent command, his companions shifted and two sets of two stacked up to become a table for a fifth woman to be draped across. Olvadi plunged into her while making disturbing eye contact with Leo.

She remained bland and motionless.

After four hours of cavorting, he finally lay down with his companions, covered in substances she didn't want to think about.

Coren came over from his post by the door. "Ambassador, we have been summoned home."

He said it loud enough for Olvadi to hear.

The vampire lifted his head from the breast of one of his creatures, and he scowled. "Go. Tell Matthias that he picked an icy bitch for his ambassador. Well done."

She inclined her head and rose to her feet. "Thank you for your hospitality, King Olvadi."

Coren wrapped her in the cloak and helped her cross the slippery floor.

It was difficult to keep a stately pace when she wanted to run all the way back to Redbird City.

When they made it to the SUV and Leo was settled in the back, Lima hugged her. "You did incredibly well, Ms. Wicks."

"I am so happy. Just one stop I would like to make before we go home. Well, two. I would like a burger for the flight home, but I need to see Octavia. I think I can wake her up early."

Coren picked up his phone and made a call. "Yes to the burger, and we will be taken straight to Octavia."

"Okay. I need a pin and some bathroom tissue."

Coren frowned but didn't mention his confusion if he felt any. "Not a problem."

Leo pulled out her phone and smiled at the image of Melody's baby face looking out at her from behind the display. It was definitely the highlight of her evening.

The short trip to Regick's home let her get her emotions back under control, and when she exited the vehicle with Lima and Coren at her side, she felt the cool expression wash over her features again.

Zora and Leah met them next to the elevators and rode up with them. Octavia was ensconced in one of the apartments on the upper floors.

Leo sat next to her and followed an impulse

that had been nagging at her. She touched Octavia's forehead and closed her eyes.

Centuries of pain and fear were working in Octavia's mind. Enchanted and sacred objects had been used to defile her body, and while Zora had offered cosmetic changes, the original scars were still there.

Leo gave her calm. She gave her the sense of the future, and she whispered of freedom to move, travel and see the sun once again. Octavia's hungry mind latched onto the thoughts eagerly.

Leo smiled and rose to her feet. When she was out in the living room again, she asked Leah, "Did you bring the pin and the tissue?"

Zora produced the objects. "What are they for?"

"When I am gone, wait an hour and then press this against her tongue. It will speed her healing." Leo stabbed her fingertip with the pin and pressed the tissue to the single drop welling there.

Leah scowled. "Will that do it?"

Leonora shrugged. "It should. I am new at this, but it should be enough to bring her around."

Zora cocked her head. "Why wait?"

"I am not a mother duck. When she looks for another vampire to bond to and doesn't find one, she will begin to become self-sufficient again. If I was here, she would follow me back to Matthias."

She handed the tissue to Zora, who carefully held it to dry the blood drop.

Leo stuck her finger in her mouth and sucked until she closed the wound. When she was done, she smiled. "This has been most interesting, but I am eager to be getting home."

Zora nodded. "Of course. Just one thing."

Leo was caught in a hug, and she returned it, careful not to accidentally stain Zora's dress with blood. "It was nice meeting you, too, Zora. Daughter of dragons."

Zora grinned. "I suspected you would see that. Well, come along. Your helicopter is waiting."

With a sense of relief, she followed her hostess up to the top floor, and she shook Regick's hand again before entering the aircraft. When the blades whirred and Lima handed her her cheeseburger, everything was right with the world.

They cruised across the sky and headed home, losing the hour they had gained on the way.

When they approached the manor and settled down, Leo fought the urge to sob with relief. The last two days had been the most terrifying in her life.

She left the helicopter with the blades still whirring and headed for the manor.

Leo entered the entryway when Dorn opened the door.

He scowled. "Ms. Wicks, you look—"

She held up a hand. "Not in the mood for it, Dorn. Matthias picked this outfit so I wouldn't be out of place at a vampire orgy, and I want to know why he didn't warn me. Is he in his office?"

"His quarters." Dorn shocked her by giving her a slight smile. "Give him hell."

Leo nodded, checked his schedule on her phone and noted that he wasn't in conference with anyone. She straightened her shoulders and stalked through the house until she reached his door.

Three brisk knocks brought an answering, "Come in."

Leo opened the door and stepped inside, looking for her tormentor.

"Ah, Leonora. Come in and tell me about your journey."

He was sitting on the couch with his feet up on the coffee table, a position so blissfully casual that she nearly forgot he was an ancient being.

She stalked in and dropped to the far edge of the couch and glared at him.

He flicked his gaze toward her. "Was there something you wanted to tell me?"

"Why didn't you warn me that Olvadi was a pervert?"

She unclasped her cloak but left it in place while she crossed her arms and glared at him.

He looked up from the tablet he was reading, and he sighed. "I didn't want to frighten you."

"I wasn't frightened; I was irritated. He kept looking at me like I was either naked or edible." She grimaced. "Or both."

"Did he make any improper advances toward you?"

She thought about being pinned to the wall with Olvadi's hand heading toward her crotch. "You could definitely say that."

Matthias sat up and he was vibrating with tension. "What did he do?"

"Pinned me up against the wall and groped me. That was when the bonding kicked in and I was able to take care of myself. The rest of his behaviour I would simply consider to be bad taste."

"Tell me everything." He moved closer to her on the couch, and she started talking.

An hour later, she was sitting and sipping the tea that Dorn had brought for her.

"So, back in the helicopter and here I am." She finished the tea that was laced with herbal sedatives. The valerian was rather distinct.

"Are you calmer now?"

She smiled slightly. "Sedated but calmer. Is Coren still on duty?"

"No, why?"

"I need him to get me out of these clothes. I have no idea how they are stuck together."

"Take off your cloak and turn your back. I am sure I can figure it out."

Leo was a little nervous, but she slid the cloak from her shoulders and pivoted so her back was facing him.

"I have no doubt that your skin proved an irritating temptation for Olvadi." Matthias pressed a cool kiss to her bare shoulder.

She shivered as his fingers trailed over the skin of her back that wasn't covered by leather or laces.

"Um, why irritating?"

"Because one mark on your skin would have meant war, and he knew it." He pressed a kiss to the opposite side of her neck.

She had been swimming in much deeper waters than she had thought.

His fingers stroked the laces, and the bodice loosened in a sudden shift. She hung on for her dignity and hoped that she would be able to manage the skirt.

"Thank you."

"You are not done yet. Your skirt and shoes are tied with the same knot."

She bit her lip and turned sideways with her hand pressed to her breasts to hold the leather in place. "This is going to get worse before it gets better, won't it?"

He grinned. "I have something that will help."

Matthias got to his feet and headed to the bedroom.

Leo slumped over and took a few deep breaths. It was more than she needed to let herself sleep.

Chapter Thirteen

Leo woke wearing Matthias's shirt and nothing else. The odd part was that she was not in her own room. She clapped her hand over her eyes when she realized she now considered that the *odd part*.

Dorn came in with a tray and set it near the bed. "Matthias said you were awake, so Lima got this for you."

A tray of oatmeal, fruit salad and toast was sitting next to a carafe of coffee. Cream and sugar were on the tray next to the mug.

"That was sweet of her."

"If you are getting up, I will let the housekeeper know that she can make the bed."

She waved at him. "I am up; I am up."

He paused. "You did excellent work in Arbor. You got in and out without causing an incident. Frankly, I didn't think you had it in you."

Leo laughed. "Thanks for the vote of confidence, Dorn. I look forward to your stern disapproval later."

"You know you have it, Ms. Wicks." He gave her a surprising smile, and he left her to her breakfast.

She flipped the sheet back and headed to the small table. First things first. She needed her breakfast.

The coffee was hot and rich. Her toes curled happily as she sipped it before diving headlong into the rest of the meal.

She ate with one hand while she checked the schedule with the other. Her phone had been conveniently near her hand when she got out of bed. Leo glanced back at the bed and saw two distinct dent marks in the pillows. Unless she had travelled from one end of the huge span to the other, Matthias had spent some time with her.

The thought was as intriguing as it was disturbing.

Her agenda was remarkably clear, but she got up and headed to her room for a shower and a change of clothing. She might think she had nothing to do, but until she checked her desk, she wouldn't know for sure.

Leo stretched in the shower, turning so that every inch of her person was scrubbed. After time in Arbor, she desperately wanted to shed her outer layer of skin.

She wandered through her large closet in her towel and picked a deep-blue work dress for the day.

To her amazement, her phone rang. It was odd to think of it as a phone.

"Hello?"

"Leo? The mayor called and told me you had the day off and that you were supposed to come over for a visit. Are you up for it?"

"You are sure it was the mayor?"

"Yes, he said that after your situation yesterday, you might want friendly faces. What is he talking about?"

"I am just going to check on that and I am going to be right over if that is all right?"

"Of course! My house is your house." Minny chuckled.

"See you in an hour."

Leo took the blue dress back to the closet and found jeans, a soft blouse and some flats. It looked like Dorn had replaced her entire wardrobe one piece at a time.

The clothes she put on were worth more than she made in a week, but they fit, so Leo wore them.

When she was dressed and her hair was braided, she headed to the office and found a large note on her desk. *Spend the day with your sister. I will call if I need you.*

Well, that was the confirmation she needed. She got her purse from the drawer where it seemed to magically return to, tossed in her phone and chucked in the summoner.

With her purse over her shoulder, she walked out to find Dorn. She found him in the kitchen with Lima.

"Hiya, Lima. Hello again, Dorn. Can you tell me where my car is? My old purse was in it, and I need some cash for tonight. I get to spend time with my sister, and I want to order in."

"Why can't your sister pay?" Dorn scowled.

"Because she is a single mother raising a daughter. Her money is for her family."

He sighed, and Lima grinned as he led the way out of the kitchen, outside via a subtly placed entrance and, from there, into a garage.

Her sad little car was sitting in a corner, surrounded by large luxury vehicles. Leo opened the passenger door and opened her purse. She grabbed her wallet and credit cards, dropping them into her new purse. Her keys were dangling from the ignition, so she snapped off the house keys and left the vehicle keys where they were, stained with blood like the rest of the interior.

"Why do you need those keys?"

"They are for my sister's house."

"Didn't she have the locks changed after the first night?"

Leo blinked at the thought. "I have no idea. I will have to ask her."

Dorn nodded. "Do. It is a little-enough thing to do but vitally important."

"You are absolutely right. Sorry, I have been a bit distracted lately."

He laughed. "I believe you have a right to be. You are coping well and not nearly as invasive as I had first thought."

"I am so glad. How do I get to the front rotunda from here?"

"Follow me."

She stuck her hand in her purse and pressed the call button. When she fished it all the way out, it had three minutes on the clock.

She followed Dorn.

They arrived by the front entryway seconds before the car pulled up.

Dorn inclined his head. "Enjoy your visit."

"I think I will."

She looked at Nathaniel and noticed that there was a subtle difference to him. A suspicion for his around-the-clock service was starting in her mind.

"Good afternoon, Nathaniel." She smiled as he held the door for her.

"Good afternoon, Ms. Wicks." He winked and closed the door when she was settled.

"I am going to my sister's place."

"And I shall be glad to take you there."

He put the car in gear, and they glided around until they were at the gate. He checked them out, and they were soon cruising familiar city streets.

It felt good to have her wallet and identification with her again. It made her feel like more of a person and less of a tool that Matthias could use as he pleased.

Yes, she had gotten herself into this situation, but the alternative had been too horrific to imagine.

She tried to imagine what Melody looked like now. It had been less than a week since she had seen her, but babies grew so fast.

When Nathaniel pulled into her sister's driveway, Leo could barely contain herself. She yelled, "Thank you," as she bolted out of the car and charged up the steps.

Antony waved at her as she waited for an answer to her knock on the front door. Minny came to the door with Melody on her shoulder, and Leo didn't know which one to hug first. She settled for both.

She hugged Minny and Melody carefully and felt a warm satisfaction run through her.

"Come on, Minny. Let's have a seat and you can tell me all about your day."

"Only if you tell me first. I saw the paper. What were you wearing?"

Leela came out of the laundry room with a basket filled with small bits of clothing. She sat down and started folding them. "Do you mind if I am in here while you chat?"

Leo shook her head. "I don't mind. You are family now. I am sure Melody has puked on you and that is equivalent to an initiation."

They all laughed, and Leo got to hold her niece while she talked about the more public points of her new job.

Minny's eyes were huge. "A vampire orgy? And you just had to sit there?"

"I didn't *have* to sit there. Trust me. I wanted to be very still in a room full of predators. Oily, horny predators." She made a face.

"Speaking of predators, what is the mayor like?" Minny bit her lip, and her eyes were gleaming.

"Not for you, Minny." Leela laughed. "Vampire rules. No children."

The mood suddenly dropped like a rock. Leo wrinkled her nose. "Yeah, that one we know. Speaking of that, has there been any disturbance recently?"

Minny reflexively reached for Melody. "Every few nights the guys tell us that there have been vampires sighted, but nothing ever comes of it."

"Right. Well, speaking of humans and what makes us different, does anyone want some takeout? My treat." She waggled her brows.

Minny chuckled. "You mean Matthias's treat. I have accepted too much already."

Leo was hurt. "I meant my treat. I went into the car and got out my wallet and cards for this."

Leela cocked her head. "They kept it?"

Leo sighed. "For now. There is too much blood in it for it to be anything but a write off. Even my purse had to be scrapped, but I was able to salvage some of the contents."

Minny frowned. "I didn't mean to insult you, Leo. Leela made some stew and that was our current plan for dinner."

Leo nodded. "Right. Well, I don't want to mess with your routine. It's important."

Minny frowned. "You should stay for dinner."

"It's all right. I am sure that I can convince my driver to stop at Taco Taco Taco!"

"You will be eaten inside out if you stop at that place." Minny scowled.

"Don't worry about it. I am made of sturdier stuff than I was last week."

She hugged everyone goodbye, even Leela. With the sun still bright, she decided that a walk might just clear her head.

The knock on the door after dinner surprised Minny. "Maybe Leo came back for dessert."

She opened the door and stared up at the seven-foot wall of icy muscle that was the Mayor of Redbird City. "Mayor Matthias."

He inclined his head. "Minuet Wicks, I have come to offer you a new home nearer the manor house."

Minny's eyes widened. "What?"

"I wish you to be closer to Leonora. She misses you and your child with an intensity that is distracting to both of us."

Minny looked back at Melody in Leela's arms. "Leo didn't say anything."

Matthias pinched the bridge of his nose. Minny was amazed; it looked just like when Leo did it.

"Please come in and have a seat."

He inclined his head and walked into the room, his head only a few inches from the ceiling. Leo had been right. He wasn't for her. He was scary.

"I don't want to move."

He waved that away. "You would not have to do a thing, and you would be moved into an area with the finest schools and playgrounds, within walking distance for your sister."

Melody started wailing. Minny reached out and took her daughter, but Melody didn't want to be calmed. Her little fists stuck out, and her face turned beet red as she howled. This was definitely a new behaviour.

"Please hand her to me. I wish to continue this discussion."

Minny could barely hear him over Melody's screaming, so she handed her over. The baby quieted so quickly she gave herself the hiccups.

Matthias held Melody comfortably and rocked

her lightly in his arms.

"Why are you so concerned for my location?"

He shrugged and Melody giggled. "If you are closer to the manor, it will be less of a commute for all of my staff, including your sister. Also, the grounds that you have here are difficult to ward sufficiently. While your lover and his maker have left the city for now, they will be back soon, and your safety is what is purchasing your sister's cooperation. I would not be pleased if Leo were to leave my service."

Minny finally began to put it together. "You have a thing for my sister."

The vampire king and Mayor of Redbird City looked at her and smiled slightly. "It has not been called a thing in centuries, but if your sister finds her way into my bed, I would be very happy to have her there."

"So you haven't..."

"No. Nor will I until she comes to me of her own will. Unfortunately for me, the world is currently moving at a wild pace. I have not been able to apply my considerable charms to wooing her."

Leela was staring at him. "You think she will stay?"

Minny was surprised by the nanny's comment.

"She will stay. I can feel it. I just have to make everything conducive to that situation. That includes moving her niece into my neighbourhood."

Minny tried one final stopping block. "There are no houses available on that block."

He smiled tightly. "You are correct. I purchased the property next to the manor this afternoon. You will be moving in two days. Pack what you need immediately and the rest will be brought by secured movers."

"Do I have a choice?"

He looked down at the baby in his hands. "This child means more to Leonora than her life, her dignity and her freedom. You have no choice. You will honour her sacrifice."

He stood and handed the baby back to Minny. Melody had her fist to her lips, and she was staring at Matthias.

Minny looked at his face and the stone-cold determination that he was radiating. There was going to be no arguing with him on this matter, and she only had one question for him.

"Is the house mine?"

He smiled, a slow grin that took over his features and blazed his triumph. "It belongs to Leonora, but she will sign the agreement to let you have it, rent free."

"She doesn't know?"

"No. I wish her settled, and that means you must be settled." He reached into his jacket and pulled out keys and a slip of paper. "Here you go. This is your new address and the security code is the year of Leonora's birth."

Minny stood with her baby in one arm and the keys and address in the other.

Leela smiled. "It looks like Melody gets to grow up in a better part of town."

Melody getting to grow up was what had started this to begin with. Minny looked at the keys and smiled. Leo had a boyfriend.

Chapter Fourteen

Her throat was burning, her stomach was in shock and the soda did nothing. Leo smiled at the familiar feeling of the taco burn in her belly.

She was wadding up her wrappers and walking across the lot when an SUV pulled up and disgorged three XIA agents and a young woman.

Leo wiped her hands and dropped the parcel into the trash bin where a troll was obviously in residence. He rumbled, and she wished she had left more for him.

She smirked at her own fanciful thoughts and pressed the summoner. Now was the test to see if Nathaniel or his doppelgangers could find her without knowing where she was in advance.

Leo checked the timer and smirked at the seven minutes. She watched the group and saw the woman speaking to the goblin running the grill, and he looked past her before returning to work. Taco Taco Taco! Catered to every species, which was nice for Leo on occasion, but the spices were gruelling if she tried it more than twice a week.

The XIA agents were watching the woman with them closely, and Leo focused on them for a moment. They were a vampire, a lion shifter and an elf with a woman who looked human but definitely wasn't. She had their undivided attention, and it seemed she didn't even know it.

Leo watched them for a few more minutes until the black car cruised up silently. Nathaniel got out and opened her door.

"Where to, Ms. Wicks?"

"Back to the manor, please. I will take a walk in the gardens and rearrange my closet to drive Dorn insane." She smiled slightly.

"You don't want to go out with friends?"

She pursed her lips as he closed the door for her. "I don't have any friends. I always did the working in the family."

"Where are your parents?"

She chuckled. "They split. Neither of them were fans of being parents, so the moment I was old enough to take custody of Minny, I did and they divorced, going their separate ways."

She shrugged. "They wanted to start again, and I think they did."

He nodded. "That does explain your loyalty to your sister."

"I am just a loyal person by nature. Even to my employers, if you can imagine that."

"I can imagine it."

"So, are you a twin, a triplet or a doppelganger of some sort?" She blurted it out.

Nathaniel chuckled. "Mind bonded triplets. Two of us are on duty at any given time."

"Are you lying to me?"

"Maybe a little."

She frowned at him. "I am going to figure this out."

He winked at her in the mirror. "Good luck with that."

She laughed and settled in her seat as he drove her back to the manor. Time for a single girl's night in.

Leo got a glass of white wine and went for a walk in the Night Garden.

She followed the path to the centre of the maze and took a seat beside the fountain. She sipped at her wine and looked around at the glowing flowers. The moon was rising above her, and she felt still inside for the first time in a long time.

She set the wine down next to her and crossed her legs, putting her palms up on her knees. She inhaled deeply and drank in the night.

Leo sat there for hours, simply letting her thoughts drift and blow in the psychic winds.

When she opened her eyes, she wasn't alone. Matthias was sitting across from her and watching her with the gaze of a lazy predator.

"I gave you the night off."

She smiled. "I took it. I went to visit Minny, had dinner and came home again."

"You didn't stay with your sister all evening?"

Leo shrugged. "I don't fit her life like I used to. She has Leela for the stuff she needs. I am superfluous now."

He was on his feet. "Did she insult you?"

Leo laughed. "No. She is my sister and has just become a mother. She is getting her priorities in order, and simply managing day to day is her focus. I can commiserate. I am in the same position."

Matthias walked to her and held out his hand. He pulled her slowly to her feet. "If I had known you were out here alone earlier, we could have spent a few hours together."

She swayed against him and smiled. "Yes, you probably have somewhere you have to be."

"But nowhere I would rather be." He leaned down to kiss her.

Leo went up on her toes to meet him. He slid a hand under her braid and held her while they kissed.

He was so careful with his teeth that she smiled at the sweetness of the kiss. The kiss turned savage, and still, he didn't draw blood.

Leo felt her feet swaying and Matthias's arms around her, holding her off the ground and against him. Her skin got hot, and she shivered in his arms. She clutched at his neck and held on as he bent her back with the ruthless intensity of his mouth.

Leo clawed at his shirt, trying to get some skin-to-skin contact. It wasn't the smooth, choreographed seductions that she had seen in Arbor, but it was working just fine for her.

Matthias lifted his head, swung her firmly into his arms, and he leaped through the air, landing thirty metres away, next to the altar stone.

His voice was gravelly as he spoke, "I had intended a more comfortable venue for our first time. If you have any objections, speak them now."

"I have no objections. It is the perfect spot."

She smiled and pushed free of his embrace, kicking off her loafers, unsnapping her jeans and peeling out of them before she wrenched her shirt over her head and dropped it on top of the pile.

In her bra and panties, she hopped up on the edge of the stone. "The rest is up to you."

He undressed more completely than she had.

Leo took in his hard and perfect form, the dark crowning of hair around his groin and the smooth shaft of his erection. He stepped between her thighs and parted her knees.

Instead of touching her between her thighs, he rubbed the small mark he had left on her inner thigh. She felt a surge of heat, and her body sent out a welcome. Leo stared up into Matthias's eyes while he licked his thumb and then rubbed that spot again.

Coils and waves of heat were coming off that small caress. Leo gripped the sides of the stone and held tight as she got closer and closer to her body and mind shattering in a blast of light and heat.

Matthias spoke in an ancient language, and he hooked a finger under the centre of her bra, slicing through it. He did the same with the panties until it fell away from her skin.

He bent his head to her breast and rubbed his lips over her skin. She moaned and held his head with one hand. His fingers moved from the point on her skin and slid inside her. The ease with which he had sliced through her clothes made her a little wary of having those digits inside her, but she moaned and moved her hips against him, trusting that no harm would come to her.

Her breath sawed in and out of her lungs, and her mind clung to reality with a desperate intensity. Reality, at this moment, was fucking amazing.

He moved and pushed her back, peeling off her panties and shoving her bra down her arms, pinning them against her sides.

She watched him as he rubbed his body across hers and the heat from her skin welcomed his cool, silken caress. Leo looked up as he pressed her to the stone, and she whispered, "I would really like you inside me right now."

His eyes glowed and illuminated the world around them. She held him as he set himself in her opening and slowly forged inside.

The difference in their body temperatures was yet another stimulus to throw onto the fire.

He moved into her, and she raised her hips. He thrust, she rose to meet him, and soon, they were rocking together with a specific goal in mind. Leo kept her gaze fixed on his as she realized that he was seeking her pleasure only.

She fell into his gaze, her mind lost to what was going on inside her. She saw stars burn in the night sky and fade while she watched. Cities rose and fell, and entire civilizations were wiped off the Earth while she watched.

Leo screamed and Matthias caught it in his mouth, swallowing her shrieks and cries as she was overwhelmed through all her senses.

Fire raged through her nerves, and it was when she felt the throbbing of her cock that she came to grips with the symbiosis of the senses that had taken place. The release of his-her cock into his-her body was a riot of sexual finality that confirmed one thing for Leo's conscious mind. She would never have another lover like this. It was probably a good thing. She might just go insane with the one she had now.

Leo relaxed in his embrace as her body went limp. His kiss went from capturing her sounds to a gentle stroking of his lips against hers.

He started to whisper against her lips and cheeks, ancient words from long-dead civilizations. She closed her eyes and let the words spark images in her mind of places she could never visit, races that had long passed. Other lovers' faces passed in her thoughts—men, women, groups of both. They gave willingly.

When he parted their bodies, she gasped at being alone in her mind again. She opened her eyes, and he was smiling down at her.

"Hello, Leonora."

"Hello, Matthias."

He lifted his hand in the air and made a peculiar gesture. A light and glowing sheet descended in his grip. He wrapped it around her with the utmost of care.

"Where did you learn how to do that?"

"One does not live as long as I have and not pick up some magic."

When she was covered, he lifted her in his arms and walked back to the house with his own assets completely on display.

He took her to his rooms and not hers. A large tub was already nearly full with steaming and scented water.

"Don't you have a meeting tonight?" Putting work in the midst of their current intimacy seemed safe.

"I rearranged it." He set her on her feet, stripped off the silken sheet and held her hand, gesturing for her to get in the tub.

Leo stepped in, he followed suit, settling behind her, and then, after a kiss to her buttocks, he tugged her down in his lap.

His cool skin soon took on the heat of the water around them, and she picked up that this was a fairly good way not to freak out your lovers.

Things had gone a little differently with her. She remembered every inch of his cool skin inside her moving with savage enjoyment of her body.

"So, are we going to discuss what just happened?" It was easy to ask him that question while her back was to his chest and he was slowly running his hands over her breasts.

"I wanted you; you wanted me. We met in the middle with enthusiasm." He pressed a kiss to her neck.

"You didn't bite me."

"You are not food." He stroked his hands over her slowly, as if memorizing her skin.

He wasn't wrong. She certainly didn't think of herself as edible.

"Oh, you now own the home next door, complete with gated grounds and maintenance personnel."

She turned in his arms, splashing as the water moved around her. She put her hands on his shoulders and held him still. "You are kidding me."

His smile was smug. "I am not. It would ease your mind to have your family closer, and the neighbours were interested in the offer I gave them. Minuet, the baby and her guards will all be moved over within the next few days. It will be easier to protect them if they are nearby."

She bowed her head. "I am going to be working for you for eternity."

Matthias lifted her chin on two fingers. "Would that be so bad?"

She stared at him and answered honestly. "I don't really know."

She leaned in and kissed him, just a simple kiss, but it seemed like she was sealing a silent contract.

When she turned again and settled against him, Leo couldn't think of another place she wanted to be in that moment.

He pressed another kiss to her neck, and his hands wandered again. It was quite entertaining considering that her original plan for the evening had been a glass of white wine in the gardens. This was much more fun.

Chapter Fifteen

Leo sat in her room and tried to decide what to do with the rest of the night. Some emissary or something had hauled Matthias away from their idyll. Leo had returned to her room to ponder the change in their connection.

He was definitely handsome, but she wasn't used to anyone pursuing her, let alone catching her. She was conflicted.

Her phone chirped, and she went to check the message. The XIA were calling in representatives. There was an event in the park.

Leo checked her face in the mirror and sighed at the silvery-grey cast to her skin. She would have it until she ate or the sun came up, whichever came first.

Well, she was already up for the night. She may as well go and represent the mayor's office. If the XIA was coming through on her phone, it must be important.

She didn't think about it. She pinned back her hair and got dressed. She had too much energy to try and stay in the manor.

She called for Nathaniel and gave him the address. She settled in silence while she waited for their arrival.

"You are quiet tonight, Ms. Wicks."

"You are formal. Sorry. My mind is a thousand miles away."

"You look a little..."

"I am grey. I know it. It will be fine. Just one of the side effects of being his apprentice, or so Matthias tells me."

"Ah. It is a good look for you. The colour suits you."

She fought a grin. The sick feeling in the pit of her stomach warned her that tonight wasn't going to be a good night.

When they approached the park, it was obvious where they needed to be. Light flooded one corner of the park and that was where Nathaniel took her.

He parked next to the XIA vehicles, and he looked at her in the mirror. "I am coming with you, to keep anyone from interfering."

"Thank you, Nathaniel."

He got out and opened her door. He walked next to her, staving off the agents and officers who were trying to slow her down.

She headed to the centre of the light, as if pulled there by something. She sniffed the air and smelled something acrid.

To her surprise, she saw the group of XIA agents and the woman who had been at the taco truck.

Before she knew what she was saying, Leo asked, "Who are you?"

The woman swallowed and showed her badge.

"I am a special observer with the XIA."

B. Ganger. Leo made a mental note.

Leo inhaled again, this time focusing on the woman in front of her. "You smell like blood."

"There was a car accident earlier. I am sure that my jeans and shoes are covered in it."

Leo observed, "There is none on your shirt."

"I changed my shirt, but I had three XIA agents rifling through my living room, so I left it at that. Tomorrow, I will bring a full change of clothing, though I have no idea where I would change."

Leo could definitely understand strange men rummaging through her personal space. She smiled brightly, and the young lady stared at her in shock, jerking back slightly.

Leo inclined her head and went to seek out the body and the coroner for details on what had happened. The coroner was checking the temperature, and Leo and Nathaniel stood nearby until the time of death could be estimated.

Leo couldn't shake the acrid scent in her nostrils. "How long has she been dead?"

The coroner looked at her in surprise. The zombie hadn't heard her approach. "I am guessing she has been dead for three hours. Magic has skewed the exact timeline. It could have been earlier or later."

Leo could feel Matthias watching from behind her eyes. "I see. I will keep the mayor informed."

"Thank you, Miss..."

"Wicks. Leonora Wicks. I am the mayor's assistant and his apprentice. I will be attending any of these events as they occur."

Nathaniel whispered the names of the folks she was about to return to. Agent Argyle was a vampire under Matthias's control. Beneficia Ganger was descended from the greatest vampire hunter ever known.

Leo walked up to them and inclined her head. "It was pleasant meeting you, Beneficia Ganger. Agent Argyle, there will be a mage team going over this place with seers. Make sure that it isn't compromised."

She could see the surprise in his eyes as he nodded and muttered. "Yes, Miss Wicks."

Leo grimaced and stuck her tongue out at him.

Benny chuckled. "It was nice to meet you, Miss Wicks."

Leo winked "Call me Leo. It is short for Leonora. I am sure I will see you again, Miss Ganger."

She turned and walked away with Nathaniel ahead of her, opening the car door as she approached. She settled in the car and tried to forget what she had seen.

The young woman looked a lot like Beneficia. She had been magically tortured and a brand had scorched the skin at the back of her neck.

Leo breathed slowly and controlled herself as much as she could. She picked up her phone and used her thumbs to tap in a report, letting Matthias know that there was a fresh demon kill in the park and the XIA were investigating.

She knew he would head out to confirm it, but that was his business. The dead woman had done what hours of sex with Matthias had been unable to accomplish. She was exhausted.

Her sister texted her and asked her to come by as soon as she could.

Matthias texted and told her he would look into the death as soon as he finished with the emissary.

Leo really needed something positive, so she whispered, "Nathaniel, take me to Minny's place, please."

"Of course. On our way."

It was three in the morning, but with the hours Leo was keeping, she didn't think that it was that peculiar.

Nathaniel pulled up to the house, but there weren't any lights on.

Leo whispered, "I really wish I had my bat right now."

Antony came out of the darkness, and he asked, "What is it?"

"I got a text from Minny. She told me to come over right away."

A harsh laugh sounded from the street. "You always were gullible, Leo."

Robert stood there, and he waggled a phone in his hand. The scent of fresh blood wafted toward them, and Leo looked toward the house.

Antony shook his head. "They are fine, Leo. No one has touched them."

Leo walked down the drive toward the road. "What do you want, Robert?"

"You know what I want. I want that baby dead so that I can claim my rightful place with my queen and rule this territory at her side."

Leo cocked her head. "A queen in charge of the territory? Really? How interesting. I thought that the vampire king was firmly in charge."

"That is what he thinks. She is massing an army, and soon, he will be a bloody pulp beneath her feet." He jerked his chin up.

"With you by her side if you can kill a helpless baby." Leo nodded. "Brave of you."

"You don't know how powerful I have already become while you whore yourself for protection."

"How many lives did your power cost, Bobbie?" She knew he hated the nickname, and she waited for a response.

He grinned, bloody teeth and fangs showing. "Not enough."

Leo stepped off the property, and he rushed at her. She struck him with an uppercut, elbowed him in the ribs and kneed him in the jaw when he knelt at her feet. He vomited blood across the asphalt, and she struck at him over and over, her rage at the death of the woman earlier in the night riding her. She beat at him until she heard the crunching of bone under her shoes and Nathaniel pried her away.

"Easy, Ms. Wicks. He is down and the property is protected. I will take you home."

"Okay. Home sounds good." She let Nathaniel put his arm around her and lead her to the car.

She sat numbly on the drive home. If only she had a weapon, she would have taken his head off.

Matthias met her car when they arrived at the manor. She was covered in blood and white as a sheet, but he lifted her bloody knuckles to his lips and kissed her. "Welcome home, Leonora."

She looked at him, but her mind was numb. "I

need a shower."

"You do. Allow me to take some photos and remove your clothing."

"Okay." She was shut down inside. She followed him inside and stood where he asked, letting Dorn take pictures of her before she went to her room and handed Matthias her clothing. She heard him say something about gene typing the blood, but she wanted a shower.

She stood in the centre of the shower blasts and watched the water go from red to pink as she got clean. She scrubbed herself from head to toe and then started over again.

Wrapped in her fluffy and comfortable robe, she walked into her bedroom, unsurprised to see Matthias waiting for her. He opened his arms, and she walked up to him, cuddling against him as her night caught up with her.

One tear turned to fifty, and she sobbed at the waves of frustration at coming too late and arriving unable to act. She didn't know her place in the world, and it scared her.

"I think I smelled demon tonight." She sniffled and rubbed her cheek on his chest.

"You did. You did very well. The power that you sensed, the energy coming off the area around the body, those are things that can be used to confirm the diagnosis of demon interference. I have told the XIA."

She nodded. "Good. Robert stole Minny's phone and lured me to the house. I don't know what he thought he would get out of it."

"What did he say?"

"That the queen is massing an army to destroy you."

He snorted. "She can try. She will fail."

He stroked her shoulder. "Nathaniel said that the entire battle took less than three seconds. By the time he got to you, it was over."

She lifted her head and frowned. "It took much longer than that."

"No. It didn't. Your time awareness shifted to match his. Do not worry about it. Rest now. I will be here when you wake up." He pressed a kiss to her forehead, and a wave of fatigue washed over her.

She lay back as he settled her on her bed. "Cheater."

He laughed and stroked her cheek. "Only when I need to win. Rest."

She snuggled into the sheets, and another wave of exhaustion washed over her. She decided to rest.

Matthias felt Leonora slip into unconsciousness, and his encouraging smile faded. He fought the rage that was ripping through him, and he returned to his guest with all speed.

"Please excuse my departure, Shaline. I had to attend to one of my staff."

The nest queen winced. "It is fine, my king. Was your staffer badly injured?"

He looked over the woman who had turned into a translucent creature over time, in the shadows with nothing but blood to sustain her.

He waved at her to sit across from him on the couch.

Dorn brought in a decanter of wine and served two glasses.

Matthias offered one to Shaline. "Would you care for one?"

She politely declined. "No. Thank you."

He shrugged and sipped at the dry red wine. "You are missing out. Speaking of staff, how is that new consort of yours doing?"

Shaline looked nervous. He could see her throat swallow convulsively. "He is well. It was kind of you to give him a dispensation for his offspring."

"It was the simplest solution. After all, holding to tradition can get you into all kinds of trouble." He sipped at the wine. It was a prop, but it was something the nest queen couldn't enjoy, so he made a show of being fascinated by it.

"My king, I hear that you have a new apprentice."

He smiled slightly. "Have you heard such a thing? Interesting."

"Are the rumours true?"

"Of course. It was time."

She brushed her black and silver hair over her shoulder. "What will you do if your human suffers an accident?"

Matthias leaned forward and offered her a deadly grin. "I would remove the entire line of those responsible from this earth and pave my garden path with their bones."

Shaline swallowed again. "I see. Well, my king, it has been wonderful to confirm the truce once again. May I be dismissed? The sun is coming up."

He nodded. "Of course. I always forget that the taken do not enjoy the caress of the sun. Yes, you may go. Oh and Shaline?"

"Yes, my king?"

"Make sure that when your consort is restored to a more mobile state, he learns what the traditions mean and he adheres to them. He will not be able to crawl away from another meeting with my apprentice. I will let her destroy him, and I will give her the tools to do it."

Shaline jolted and swallowed. "She is here?"

"Oh, yes. She is here and unscathed, which is good for you, as I am aware of your attempt to distract me while your consort lured her to an ambush." He released the leash he kept on his power and pressed down on the nest queen. "Do not think that you can depose me, Shaline. It is not the first time a taken has had that idea. I destroyed the one who spawned your line, and I will not hesitate to remove parasites from what remains."

Shaline bowed low and backed away; she didn't respond. She couldn't. Matthias kept the pressure on her throat until she had reversed herself to the entryway.

The moment that he released her, she darted away at full speed.

Dorn came out of the shadows, and he asked, "Do you think that she got the hint?"

"Oh, I think that she caught on. It will take her days to repair her beau, and in the meantime, Leonora can begin training."

"I do not think she will enjoy that."

He chuckled at the understatement. "I do not care. For her safety, I want her able to drive any vehicle and use any weapon. Magic is off limits to her, so that leaves everything else."

He returned to Leonora's side and undressed, crawling into bed with her. Her heartbeat sounded deafening in the dark room, and he let it lull him into the closest thing he could feel to sleep.

Chapter Sixteen

"Leo, I love you, but your boss is really highhanded." Minny sat with Leo in the front yard and watched the moving vans bring everything she owned through the heaviest wards money could buy.

"Yes, but he is the mayor and does get what he wants." It had been thirty-six hours since the fight with Robert, and Leo was back to normal, more or less. Her skin tone was back to pink.

"He came in and talked to me, you know." Minny looked over to where Leela was playing with the baby.

"The mayor? Odd. He is not normally chatty." Leo smiled.

"It might have been a dream, but I remember his eyes glowing as he spoke to me. He said that you had done more than just take the job with him. You had attacked a vampire queen."

Leo shrugged. "She is a nest queen who is getting above herself. She came in search of Robert. She was the one who chewed on me."

"I don't remember much from that night. Robert came to the door, and then, he lunged at me with those fangs." She shuddered. "I can't imagine one of those blood fans letting themselves be bit."

Leo shrugged. "It takes all kinds."

Minny leaned in close and whispered. "You haven't let him..."

Snorting with laughter, Leo looked at her sister. "I haven't let him do anything. What I have done was necessary." She paused and answered honestly, "And some was for fun."

Minny ducked her head to ensure privacy. "And he drinks from you?"

The cool feeling of his hair against my inner thighs and the steady motion of his tongue...

Leo cleared her throat as her blush burned her cheeks. "Not after I got the apprentice mark. Not blood."

"Then what... oh." It was Minny's turn to blush.

The movers were walking slow and steadily into the house. The zombies could lift almost anything, and they may take longer, but they didn't complain or file lawsuits if they were injured. They simply repaired themselves and got on with it.

The first moving truck was the entire contents of Minny's drawers and cupboards. Matthias had requested that the furniture remain in place for a few weeks. He had provided complete replacements for everything, plus plenty of furniture for the rest of the house.

"You know, Leo. I never thought you would be interested in a guy."

"You thought I was after girls?"

"No, you just never seemed to be interested in anything but work."

"You were always too involved in your own relationships to notice mine. I have had a few, but they were little flares, no lasting burn."

"What about Matthias?"

Leo sighed. "I am with him as long as it takes. I will keep you safe no matter the situation, by whatever means necessary."

"Will he break your heart?"

"Probably. It is more likely that I will lose it."

They watched two grey-skinned men carry a couch in under the new housekeeper's watchful eye.

Minny finally said, "You don't need to do all of this for us."

"I do. Since Mom and Dad took off, you are all I have."

Minny took her hand and squeezed it. "Not just me. Not anymore. There is Melly, too."

"Melly has you and Leela. I am just backup." Leo shrugged. "I am used to it."

"You aren't just backup. You are just so self-sufficient that I forget you need somebody to listen now and then. The other night, you needed to talk, didn't you?"

Leo nodded. "I did. It's okay. It has been resolved."

Her sister stared at her for a moment. "That was when you two got physical?"

"Um, yup. I was in the Night Garden, drinking alone, and he came in to console me. The next thing I know, we were naked." Leo shrugged as if she didn't know what had happened next.

Her phone chirped, and she sighed. "Well, enjoy the rest of moving day. I have to get to work."

"Will you be coming over later?"

"I will try to make it tomorrow morning before I pass out. Oh, you got your new phone?"

Minny blushed. "I had no idea that he had gotten it."

"Well, you have a new number, and you need to start getting it to your friends. That should take you a few days." Leo got up, and she started toward the wall that divided the two properties. A heavy door was being installed, but today, Leo could just walk through.

She crossed to the manor's property and jogged across the grounds to the main house. She had half an hour to shift into her normal business garb. French braiding her hair was going to take nearly half that time, but she didn't want to get helmet head. Today, she was learning how to ride motorcycles of differing engine sizes, in heels. She wouldn't need to ride unless it was an emergency, and if it was an emergency, she wouldn't have a chance to change. Learning how to ride in office clothing was the easiest way to make sure she could do it if necessary.

Yesterday, she had done some light fight training, and Reed was an excellent instructor. Today, Coren would show her the finer points of riding a two-wheeled vehicle. Tomorrow, Nathaniel was on schedule to teach her how to drive stick.

She passed Coren with the collection of vehicles from scooters to a motorcycle that looked like it ate lesser bikes for breakfast.

He looked at her as he arranged the vehicles,

tapping his wrist and flicking his wings.

"I am on it. Promise."

He grinned as she scuttled past him and into the manor, trying not to squeak her sneakers as she passed the deputy mayor's office. Tiptoeing at high speed was becoming something of a habit for her.

She made it to her quarters and pulled off her top and shimmied out of her jeans, pausing to yank her sneakers off.

The dress went on over her head, the shoes were practically jumped into, and she ran back to the bathroom, took a deep breath and started working on her hair.

She finished her braid in plenty of time, stuck her phone into her bra and headed out of her quarters, toward the front entryway.

"Leonora, please come here."

Matthias was sitting with a small group of people, which were obviously a family when Leo saw them together.

The man was golden and elegant, the older woman had dark hair and bright blue-green eyes, and their daughter sat between them, her blonde hair and greenish eyes showing the mix of her parents as obviously as her bone structure did.

Matthias's arm was still extended to her, so she stepped into place beside him, and he took her hand, kissing it softly.

"Leonora Wicks, these are the DeMonstres, the Cursed Ones. They are the monster hunters for the surrounding areas. Master disenchanters."

Leo smiled at the DeMonstres. "I am pleased to

meet you."

The family smiled and nodded in unison.

"Where are you off to, Leonora?" Matthias asked her casually.

"I have two hours of motorcycles before I shower and get to my normal duties."

"Ah. Coren is ready?"

"He is. He is even tapping a watch he doesn't have."

Matthias chuckled. "Have fun."

She gave him a look that said he had ordered her to learn and his snicker turned a little evil.

She turned to his guests. "It was nice to meet you."

The younger woman got to her feet. "I will walk out with you."

Matthias beckoned her, and Leo leaned in. He wrapped a hand around the back of her head and kissed her.

She blushed, and when he let her go, she cleared her throat and walked out, waiting for the young woman, who looked about seventeen years old.

The woman smiled as they left the manor. "My name is Sophia, by the way."

"Leo." Leo extended her hand, and those eyes turned brilliant emerald when they made contact.

"Wow. You are not a vampire."

"Nope."

"But you have the power."

Leo shrugged. "Do I? Good for me. So, what does being a Cursed One entail?"

Sophia grinned. "As Mayor Matthias stated, we disenchant things. Our curse is to travel whenever there is an object in the hands of someone who cannot control it. We unravel the influence and destroy the object if we can. We render it unusable if at all possible."

"Sounds like a rough gig."

Sophia chuckled. "I have been doing it for over a decade, but it has its moments."

Leo was alarmed. "How young were you when you started?"

Sophia touched her face. "Oh, this. This is part of the curse. Youth is the best monster bait there is, so the active Cursed One doesn't age much." She smirked. "Folks gave my father looks when he married my mother. It was fine when they were young, but as time went on and she looked like a teenager, he got some comments."

Coren was standing near the bikes and tapping his wrist.

Leo glanced at Sophia to excuse herself, and she noted that the blonde monster hunter was blushing as she stared at Coren.

"Um, have you two met?"

"A few years ago. I doubt he remembers, but he is so fun to look at." Sophia shook herself. "Right. I had better get inside before my parents start whipping out the hint that I need to find a man. Matthias is good at matchmaking, but I am not sure that I want one of his choosing for my boyfriend."

Leo nodded and grinned. "He does have peculiar taste."

Sophia smiled and gave her another assessing look, her eyes flicking pure green again. "He definitely chooses those who can add something to his life. He is lucky to have found you."

Leo inclined her head at the compliment. "I found him, but that is a tale I hope to tell you some day. Good afternoon, Sophia."

"Good afternoon, Leo. Have fun."

Leo straightened up and walked toward Coren. Fun was not what she was looking forward to. Healing was what came to mind.

Chapter Seventeen

After dumping two of the bikes, she got the hang of it and her arm was healed by the time she sat at her desk to work over the day's correspondence.

"You changed your dress." Matthias was grinning at her from his desk.

"Changed, destroyed, potato, potahto." She finished the response to another request for Matthias to attend the waking of a new zombie.

"Instead of training tomorrow night, how would you like to join me at the gala at the museum celebrating the new additions to their vampire history collection?"

Leo blinked rapidly. "Like... a date."

"Yes."

She thought of her options and finally smiled. "Yes. I would like that."

"Excellent. Dorn has acquired a suitable gown for you."

Leo laughed and went back to work. Apparently, she was transparent when it came to his requests. Today was for work and smiling at a few images that arrived in her email of Melody trying to eat her own toes.

The invitation to the gala wasn't on her desk. She scowled and looked over at Matthias somewhere around three in the morning. "Where is that invitation?"

He lazily reached over and lifted a heavily embossed piece of cream paper, edged with gold. "Here it is."

She got to her feet and moved stiffly across the room, "May I see it?"

"Of course." He pulled it back toward him so that she had to walk around his desk to reach for it. "It is lovely penmanship."

She reached for it, and he switched hands, holding it so that she had to lean across his body.

Leo reached, he shifted, and she ended up in his lap.

"Mr. Mayor, this is highly inappropriate during working hours."

He grinned. "I am upholding a proud tradition of men in my position."

"What?"

"Chasing my secretary." He wrapped his hand around her hip and held her close.

She laughed. "You hardly chased me."

"I am ancient and wise; I lured you in." He winked before he leaned in for a kiss.

Leo caressed his cool cheek as he teased her and got her heart pounding.

The slide of his lips against hers wasn't possessive but playful. She enjoyed the moment and the taste of his smile.

When he released her, she returned to her desk

while he left to have a meeting with representatives from the XIA and the Mage Guild.

Leo focused on his schedule and the open spot that would occur in two hours. It took a lot of self-control not to write her name in that blank spot, but she would have him to herself at the museum. The director would be terrified.

"Mayor Matthias, this is Director Simmons of the Redbird City Museum. His speciality is ancient races from before the first recorded wave. Director Simmons, Mayor Matthias."

Leo stood in her crimson silk gown with her tiny clutch holding only her cell phone and a lipstick. The car summoner was tucked into her cleavage.

They were at the preview. The formal gala would not occur for another hour. This was Matthias's opportunity to see the items he had donated in their secure settings.

At his urging, Leo kept her hand on his arm while they went through the exhibit. The director was babbling excitedly over the age and condition of the objects that had been donated. He obviously considered losing Leo a fair trade.

Security was visible around the room. It was probably a good idea as the amount of extranaturals at the gala would be exceedingly high. Off-duty Mage Guild officers and XIA agents were in definite control of the space.

Well, that explained why Matthias had met with the commanding officers the night before.

The director suddenly stopped and blurted out,

"Mr. Mayor, I must ask. Is Leo wearing the *Heart of Life?*"

Matthias inclined his head. "You have a good eye. I considered offering it to the museum, but Leonora convinced me that it would be best to remain in my collection."

She scowled and touched the necklace he had placed on her after their two hours together and before dawn that morning. "I did not say that. I merely said that you had already sent more than enough to compensate the director for my loss."

The director looked longingly at her necklace before shaking his head. "Of course, the security for that particular jewel would bankrupt the museum."

She smiled. "It is a good thing that it is on me and not behind a display case."jm

Matthias inclined his head. "Please, excuse us while we look at the rest of the exhibits. There are several items that I have not seen in centuries."

"Of course, of course." Director Simmons nodded nervously and waved at them to continue without him.

When they were out of earshot, she asked him, "You didn't think to mention that this is a necklace with a history?"

"Everything I have has a history. The central stone of the necklace and six of the stones on the sides were made with amber from the tree of life."

"Does it do anything dangerous?"

"Of course not." He stroked her cheek. "Have I told you how lovely you look this evening?"

She blushed. "You look rather striking as well. I

have seen you in a tux in the newspaper, but it is a little different to be next to you."

"Our exit from the car will be on the front of every newspaper, feature on the net and be broadcast around the globe. I was delighted to be standing next to you in those images."

"Because you have a new pet?" She kept her tone light, but he locked in place.

"You are not a pet. You are my apprentice, my companion, and one day, I hope to make our connection permanent."

Leo patted his arm. "I didn't mean to mock. I have just never seen you with anyone in this capacity in my lifetime." She looked at him and frowned. "What do you mean *permanent?*"

"You know what I mean. You are very well suited to an immortal life."

She blinked. "I am a sister and an aunty. I want to be there for them, as a human."

He smiled. "I am aware of it, but Minuet and Melody will not always need you there to catch them if they fall. Once Melody has reached adulthood, I believe she will be able to deal with her aunt being a vampire queen."

In her mind, she saw a lovely Melody getting her diploma and Matthias rising from next to Leo, bending her back and biting her in front of all and sundry.

Leo shook her head to get out of the daydream.

"So, I would go straight to queen, no messing around as a countess for a while?"

He pulled her in close and steered her to one of the displays. "You are a very funny woman. I would raise you to empress, but you would get too big for your britches."

She snorted, and they continued their tour of the exhibit as well as the museum's own collection of vampire artifacts.

The DeMonstres were in attendance, and Leo found Sophia, cornering her as soon as it was polite to do so.

"Leo, you look amazing!"

Leo blushed. "You are one to talk, you look like jailbait."

Sophia was wearing a daringly cut sapphire cocktail dress. She sighed despondently. "I know. I swear I actually saw a guy look me over and then smack himself for thinking whatever he was thinking."

Leo laughed. She couldn't help it, most women would kill to look young forever, and Sophia was cursed with it. Her mother, Lillian, and father, Gerard, had the hopeless look of those devotedly in love as they swayed to the music of the live band.

"I want to look like that one day." Leo wasn't sure if she said it or Sophia said it.

"I think you are about to have your chance." Sophia chuckled.

Leo looked in the direction that Sophia had her head turned, and Matthias was making his way through the crowd toward her.

Part of her wanted to hide, she even darted a glance around, but he was next to her in a moment.

"Leonora, would you care to dance?" He held

out his hand.

Leo's heart started pounding at the image of him, his hair sliding over his ear and just the hint of fang showing as he smiled. "I am not very good."

"You will improve with practice."

She turned to Sophia and excused herself before taking Matthias's arm and heading toward the dance area.

A few other couples were swaying together, but when Matthias took the floor, they all gave them some space.

He decorously put one hand on her waist, she placed her hand on his arm, just like she had learned in junior high, and he gently gripped her other hand in his. They swayed.

This time, it wasn't in front of a bunch of vampires who had other things on their minds. This time, he was displaying her to all members of Redbird City society. This dance was serious.

She fought her urge to sprint for the door and looked into his eyes, relaxing at his expression. He wasn't going to let her do anything stupid.

That meant more to her than she could say, and she tried to put that into her eyes.

He smiled slowly, and they began to step a little faster, turning and moving around the other dancers with the most graceful of motions. Leo enjoyed the dancing and blanked her mind to any negative thoughts about her own skills. His were enough for both of them.

She felt her tiny clutch buzz, and she ignored it. This was so much more fun.

The waltz that they were dancing was definitely seductive. She couldn't imagine trying a tango. She might melt directly into a puddle right then.

When the dance was over, they stopped and applauded the musicians with the rest of the audience. Leo smiled as Matthias kissed her hands one at a time.

The director whisked him off for some information on one of the displays, and Leo returned to Sophia. "Sorry about that. Duty called."

"And now I just hope that I find a guy I can look at like you and Matthias look at each other. That would make me ecstatic."

Leo blushed. "Was it that bad?"

"It was amazing. I think someone caught it on film." Sophia wagged her eyebrows. "I think I see the photographer. Let me go check."

Leo stood by herself and used the opportunity to check her phone. An image of her sister and Melody bound and tied together filled the screen.

The next text said, *Come alone or I kill them both.*

Leo's heart started pounding, but she turned and headed for the exit.

She pressed the summoner and checked the time. It was a zero count, which meant he was already there.

She looked around and saw Nathaniel. He was staring at the gridlock surrounding his vehicle and raising his hands in frustration.

She stalked up to him. "Nathaniel, find me any kind of vehicle. It's an emergency."

He took in her expression, and he glanced

around. "That will do."

One of the photographers had brought his motorcycle to the gala, and he was only too happy to loan the bike to the mayor's apprentice for the night, provided that she let him get one picture of her on it.

She agreed, pasted a smile on her face, straddled the bike with her dress hiked up, and when he had the pictures he wanted, Nathaniel interrupted and handed her a backpack with a familiar handle sticking out the back. She slipped it on her back, fired up the bike and roared off.

Chapter Eighteen

The photo had been taken with Minny on the old couch, so she had been lured back home.

Matthias said he had put something in place to protect the house, but he hadn't shared the details with Leo.

She drove the bike as fast as she could without ditching it and finally roared up to her sister's previous home.

She paused and removed the bat, ditching the backpack and turning off the motorcycle before heading up the stairs.

She could smell blood the moment she stepped through the door. Leo walked into the living room, and there was Robert, sitting in the leather chair, blood on his mouth and jaw, his white shirt gleaming in the darkness.

"Oh, Leo. You were late, so I had a snack. It seems I have solved my problem."

The bodies of Minny and Melody were discarded to either side of the chair, but there was something wrong.

Leo tasted the layer of magic in the home. She also knew for a fact that Minny and Melody were safe at home, because she had just gotten a midnight-feeding photo.

"Well, Robert. It looks like you ignored the pass that Matthias offered to your nest's queen."

He went from sinister sneering to slightly unsure. "What?"

"Oh, yes. She was given authorization to offer you dispensation for your offspring. You could have just left Minny and Melly alone." Her voice hitched, but it was rage and not grief.

"My queen said I had to kill them, so I did."

"Good to know. I will pass that along to Matthias. I am sure that Shaline will learn her lesson at his hands."

Robert stood and approached her. "It is convenient that you dressed for your funeral, Leo."

She saw it in slow motion. He formed claws with his hand, and he swiped at her. She didn't flinch; she lifted up the bat and caught his attack.

She let him attack. She wanted to make absolutely sure that he thought her sister was dead.

When they were out of the living room and in the dining room, she swung the bat. The lightest tap from her sent him spinning into the wall. She waited until he charged her again, and she struck him again.

He began to heal after every strike, but after the third, the healing stopped. At that point, she reached for the butcher knife that Minny had always kept under the kitchen table for defense, and as neatly as she could, she severed his head.

"Excuse me, he is dead now."

The two attacked bodies shifted, and the woman lifted the baby in her arms. "You knew we were zombies?"

"I have met with the deputy mayor a few times. I recognized the feeling. Thank you so much for your help."

The woman smiled. "Mayor Matthias gave us a good start on life after life. His only caveat was for us to wear these faces until the vampire came for us. His glamour caster was a master. Even I didn't recognize myself."

Leo nodded, and she continued to hold the head by the hair.

"Let me get you a bag for that."

In a few minutes, she had formally introduced herself to the zombie family, gotten a text from Nathaniel that he was waiting for her in the drive.

She thanked Emily and Nora before taking her bat and her party favour out of the house.

She was dripping with blood and looked at the limo with trepidation.

Nathaniel gave her the news. "Matthias is still waiting for you at the party. There is a second gown in the back of the limo, and you have twenty minutes and all the mirrors you can find to clean up."

"What do I do with the head?"

"I will take care of it."

Since there was a spare dress, she wiped herself off on the one she was wearing and crawled into the back of the limo.

She unzipped quickly, finding the wet wipes and working quickly on any part of her that would touch the new gown.

There were plenty of spots she had missed, but she would have to go back to the party and excuse herself to the ladies' room.

She wriggled into the copy of the dress, checked her necklace and did up the back buttons that kept it above her tailbone.

She still had six blocks left, so she scrubbed at her arms and hands.

When the limo pulled up, she was a little rumpled but not horribly. To her shock, Nathaniel pulled up next to the limo, riding the motorcycle.

Well, there definitely were more than one of him.

He gave the cycle back to the photographer and then helped her out of the car and into the party. She passed security and found Matthias in a moment.

She smiled slightly as she passed some shifters and a few vampires. When she reached Matthias, anyone with enhanced senses knew she smelled of blood.

He inclined his head and took her aside. "Where did you go?"

"Couldn't you feel it? I took care of Robert. Removing his head will do it, right?"

"Definitely." He frowned. "I did not feel any panic, any alarm from you."

"Probably because that is not what was going through my mind. Nice work with the zombies."

He inclined his head. "Thank you. Considering what else is going on, I was a slightly irritated when I realized you had left."

"What else is going on?"

"The nest is being destroyed. The queen had proven herself unreliable. Her view exceeded her reach."

The quiet meetings, the heavy security and the appearance of both Nathaniels was a little clearer. "I see."

"So, imagine my emotions when I found out you had left the party. I will be dealing with Nathaniel when we return to the manor."

Leo straightened. "You will not."

"You will deal with him?"

She poked him in the chest. "I went. I chose to do it. I asked him to get me a vehicle. You are the one who insisted on my learning all types of bikes. Blame yourself."

"Wow, you really took it around and aimed it at me. Nicely done." Matthias looked surprisingly amused.

"Thanks. I have worked with men before. Aiming responsibility at you seemed the wisest course."

He sighed and lifted her chin with two fingers. "You are a trial."

"And yet, you keep me nearby." She leaned up and kissed him quickly.

"I find it comforting to contain your spontaneity. It gives me something to distract myself."

She laughed and looked around. They were standing next to a sacrificial mask made of gold with the neck exposed. It was a first feeding mask of ancient vampires. They would stake down a victim, and the mask kept them from being distracted by the person they were consuming.

From what Matthias was telling her, he kept

her around because he was bored. He needed a distraction, and she was it.

Leo laughed. "Glad to be of service. Now, shall we return to your adoring public?"

"Stay at my side, or I will chain you to me the next time we go out." He pulled her against him, and she could feel every inch of his body under the fabric. Her hormones hummed to life at the contact.

"Understood." She ran her hands under the jacket of his tux.

He shivered slightly and caught her hands. "Don't tease."

"Not a tease, just a reminder that me not being chained leaves a lot of possibilities." She patted his chest and pulled her hands out.

He straightened his shoulders, she took his arm and they returned to the party.

Leo hummed some of the music in the limo on the way home. Matthias cuddled her against him and stroked her hair as the car wound its way through the nearly empty streets.

"So, where do you keep the limo?"

He chuckled. "In the same garage as the bikes. You never know when you need to make an impression."

She nodded. "I can confirm that. Well, what happens to the vampires that weren't under the queen's thrall?"

"They will be given the opportunity to join the nest of the new king or queen."

"You will invite a new vampire into your territory?"

He laughed. "I don't have time to monitor them myself. Cleaning out the nest will show my resolution. I gave her enough time to change her mind. She refused to bow to my commands. This is the price for peace."

She nodded. "So, vampire life isn't worth much to you. Good to know."

"Taken vampires are either not given a choice or become vampires in pursuit of power. Either way, they are not beings that can be trusted."

"What about Octavia?"

"Who? Oh, Regick and Zora's new addition. She is now a given vampire."

Leo cleared her throat. "She was Olvadi's second in command for years. She would be a good choice as the new queen."

"Leo, are you playing politics?"

"Maybe. Just taking it out for a spin." And Octavia was the only vampire that Leo knew with no ties to another community.

"Good idea. I will contact her in the morning. After all those years in the dark, I am betting that she gets up to watch every dawn."

They went through the checkpoint at the gate, and Nathaniel drove them up to the manor. He opened the door, and Matthias stepped out before turning to ease Leo out into the cool predawn air.

With a swift move, he lifted her in his arms and carried her into the manor. She draped her arm around his neck for balance, and he carried her into the manor with all the grace of a man who had swept more than one woman off her feet.

She whispered as he walked, "If you didn't think I would go after Robert, why did you have a second dress with Nathaniel?"

Matthias smirked, "I wanted to be prepared for any eventuality."

"Were you a boy scout?"

He chortled. "No, but I consumed an eagle scout once. That, however, is a tale for another time. For now, I am trying to be romantic."

Leo giggled at the blunt description of his motives and pressed a kiss to his cheek. Perhaps the fifth glass of champagne had been a bad idea.

It was his room tonight, and the skylight let the stars fade as the dawn crept over them.

Leo draped her arms around his neck as he knelt with her impaled on his lap. He lifted and lowered her slowly, and once again, she was spun into his past.

Songs of love ran through her mind, each as sweet as the one before. The emotion in his mind was genuine, and it was aimed toward her.

As the light around them brightened, she held onto him, clutched at him and bit him gently. It was a slow and deliberate ending to a very trying day.

Chapter Nineteen

"Leo, you are on the front of the daily paper!" Minny burst in, and Leo looked at her with bleary eyes.

Leo sat up and looked at Minny. "How did we get into my room?"

Matthias wrapped an arm around her hips and pulled her toward him. "You said you would get on top if I gave you home-court advantage."

Minny was standing in the doorway, shocked. "The butler said I could just come right in."

Dorn came in after her and brought a tray for Leo, setting it on the small table. "I included a cup for your sister, Ms. Wicks."

Leo kissed Matthias quickly, grabbed the sheet and wrapped it around her, leaving him naked.

"Sit, Minny. Tell me what you are talking about." Leo poured a cup of hot coffee and simply inhaled it for a minute.

Minny was staring at the large, naked vampire in her sister's bed.

Leo snapped her fingers. "Hello, Minuet!"

Minny nodded toward Matthias. "Naked."

"That is his problem. He is the ancient one; he

can figure out how to get dressed."

Matthias got to his feet, sauntered over to Leo and pried the sheet out of her hands. He kissed her as he pulled away her covering and wrapped it around his own hips.

He leaned back and tapped her nose with one finger. "See? I figured it out."

He wandered into her bathroom, and the shower started up.

Minny looked around and grabbed Leo's robe. "Uh, does that hurt?"

Leo looked down and spotted the bruise on her rib. "I didn't even feel it. It must have happened in the... altercation last night."

Leo slid the robe on and tied it, sitting at her tiny table. "So, what was it that you wanted me to see?"

Minny shook her head and came back to herself. "Did you see this? You are on the front page and above the fold. Is that the necklace?"

Leo touched her throat, and the necklace was still there. "Yeah, it is. Apparently, it is an ancient artifact. It took a bit for Matthias to get it on me, so I am guessing there is a catch to the catch."

"Are you reading the article?"

Mayor's New Apprentice Catalyst for War.

Leo blinked. "Oh. Well, not really."

She skimmed the article, and it said that it was her presence in the mayor's manor that had instigated the eradication of the queen's nest.

"Did you really do that? Why would you do something like that, Leo?"

Leo sipped at her coffee. "It wasn't me. The

queen wanted you dead and told Robert that he couldn't be a proper drone unless he killed you and Melody. Matthias had already authorized Melody. There was no issue. She wanted you dead, so she defied Matthias. That set a whole shit storm of events into motion."

"Why? Why did she want us dead?" Minny thudded into the chair.

Leo poured Minny a cup of coffee, adding cream and sugar.

"I am only guessing, but despite Robert being a power-hungry jackass, he loved you on some level. She had to make sure that that threat to his loyalty was stamped out." Idly, Leo wondered if his head was still in the trunk of the limo.

"So, what will happen now?"

"You and Melody are safe. Robert is dead."

She looked ill. "Are you sure?"

Leo remembered carving through his neck. "Pretty sure."

"Leo, what do you know?"

Leo sighed and told Minny about the night that Robert lured her there, the previous evening and the zombie decoys.

"I am thinking that your time with Matthias has cracked you. That sounds insane."

Leo looked around and found her little purse with her phone inside it. Dorn was good about keeping it in her room when she left it around the manor.

Leo thumbed up the picture and showed it to Minny. Her sister turned grey.

"Fortunately for my sanity, after I got that, you sent me a late-night toe-nibbling-session photo."

Leo turned the image to Minny. "So I knew you were fine."

Minny was sitting there, stunned. "Leela mentioned that you would be awake and I should start sending you stuff to get you through your work day."

"She knows her stuff. She is descended from someone in my job. Her great grandfather was an apprentice."

Minny looked at the bed. "*He* was an apprentice?"

"Yeah."

"You don't mind?"

Leo smirked. "Then was then, now is now. After me, there will be another. I am not very concerned by this."

Minny frowned. "I *am* very concerned by this."

"Why? You have spent your life seeking a man to complete you, and they have always fallen short. I was already good the way I was, and I will be fine if Matthias and I part ways, though, at this point, that is a few decades off."

"What?"

"I am on contract until Melody is out of school. Neither he nor I can back out of it."

"You..."

"I promised you two would be safe and that costs money in this world. Limross and Timorn aren't nearly as cheap as they act. Even Antony can't live on acorns."

Minny's cheeks warmed.

"Oh, seriously? All three of them?"

Minny swallowed her coffee. "Nothing has

happened, but they are interesting and interested."

"Have your stitches healed?"

Minny's shoulders sank. "Not yet. A few more days and then I have to wait until things get back to normal."

"Yeah, one would think you just had a baby."

They giggled, and the bathroom door opened, disgorging a column of steam. "Leo, could you come in here and get my back for me?"

Leo patted Minny on the shoulder. "Sorry. Work is calling."

Leo got up, kissed her sister on the forehead and headed into the bathroom. "Work, work, work."

Minny's laughter as the door closed kept the grin on Leo's face far longer than was appropriate when Matthias pinned her to the wall and slid into her, hot and wet.

She bit her lip in case Minny was still outside, but when she tried to claw her way through the glass wall of the shower, Matthias held her against him until the last shiver and shake dissipated.

Leo gasped for air, the tang of her own blood on her lips.

Matthias threaded his hand through her hair and tilted her head so that he could taste that blood. He purred happily against her lips, slid out of her and turned her around. "Good morning, Leonora."

"Good morning, Matthias. My sister knows everything."

"Good. She shouldn't be kept unaware of why you are here and what you are doing for her and hers."

"So, when I am done being your apprentice, will I get an amazing pension and be matched up with one of your allies?"

He ran his hands over her slippery back. "No. After you are ready to no longer be my apprentice, I will share everything with you. I have told you that."

"I thought you were trying to keep me calm."

"I was, but in the interest of full disclosure, you are not leaving me." He opened his mouth, and his fangs were exposed.

He leaned toward her, and she shot her hand up and held him by the nose. "I am not food."

His jaw closed with a snap. His smile was slow. "Now, you are getting it."

"If you want my blood, there is only one place you are taking it from."

His eyes brightened. "In that case..."

He lifted her and removed her from the shower, carrying her across the room and setting her on the marble counter. He knelt in front of her, parted her thighs and he bit down.

Her hands touched and held the wet silk of his hair as he sucked on her inner thigh. The sharp pain mixed with the suction, and she gasped as her body broke out in a rush of heat and a slow contraction of muscles began in time to the pull of his mouth.

She squeaked when her control broke and her mind shattered into tiny sprinkles of glitter. She slumped over him and braced herself on his shoulders.

His tongue was moving slowly against her inner thigh, closing her wound. He looked up at her and smiled. "I think we are both ready for the rest of the day now."

Matthias stood, and there was a flush to his cheeks. He wrapped a towel around his hips and winked. "I will see you this evening. We are expected at an event at the Ganger home."

"Is that like Benny Ganger?"

"Yes. It is a celebration that she has been accepted for XIA training. Little Benny has always been a tempest in a teacup. This is the first moment that folks are getting to see it. Oh, I believe that Regick and Zora will be there."

Leo hopped off the counter and tested to see if her legs would hold her. "Has Dorn picked my outfit?"

He grinned. "Probably. See you later, Leonora."

She wrapped herself in a towel and walked into the bedroom where Minny was reading a magazine.

"Is the butler a giant?"

"Dorn? Probably. I don't ask. He has a lovely eye for style."

"Really?"

"Where do you think I got all of the clothes that I have been seen in? You know my own taste runs to the simple and basic... and washable."

"Can I see the new stuff?"

Leo checked her towel and nodded. "Sure. After this, did you want to go for brunch?"

"Leela is watching Melody, so sure. I have an hour or so."

"Great. Help me pick an outfit."

She led the way into the closet, and her sister squealed, "No way!"

Minny was lost, and Leo was thankful that they weren't the same size or her clothing would be sneaking across the yard and through the gate.

Since Minny was lost in a sea of silk and designer labels, Leo went hunting for clothes that she could wear out.

Jeans, a glossy t-shirt and some underwear left with her, while Minny was holding one of the evening gowns up to herself. Out of the line of sight, Leo shimmied the panties on, dropped the towel and then slid on the bra. Her shirt and jeans rubbed against sensitive skin that had been grazed by teeth and stroked by rough hands.

She tiptoed back into her closet, and she found her sister staring at the gown Leo had worn the night before.

"This cost more than my house."

"Oh, speaking of your house, Matthias arranged for it to be sold, and the money is in your bank account. The zombies who are in there really like the neighbourhood. Oh, but your furniture has been totalled."

Minny frowned. "How?"

"Robert wrecked it." Leo smiled. "Come on; let's go for brunch before Dorn has something prepared for us."

"Ms. Wicks? Lima has prepared something for you and your guest. It will be served on the patio near the Night Garden."

Leo scowled and stamped her foot, but she said

sweetly, "Thank you, Dorn."

Minny grinned at her. "Sorry. Even your purse is worth more than my car."

She slipped on her shoes and sighed. "It is Matthias's rule. I represent him when I am out, so Dorn does my shopping and Nathaniel drives me. He doesn't want me to get a ticket or into a fender bender. Plus, this way, I can alter the schedule while I travel."

"Okay, I need to know about what you actually do for him, aside from what I walked in on." Minny snickered.

Leo grabbed her hand and hauled her out of the closet. "Come on, I will explain what I do for a living, and you can explain how you use a breast pump."

They walked through the halls with Leo pulling and Minny stopping to look at the artwork and pictures of the mayor and deputy mayor respectively.

"Come on. We are nearly to the gardens. I promise that Lima has made something fabulous."

"Who is Lima?"

Leo explained about the cook or chef of the manor as they came out to the patio where an elegantly small dining set had been arranged for them.

"Does this happen often?"

"That stuff appears so I don't have to leave? Yeah. I am guessing that Matthias can keep better track of me if I am nearby."

Minny settled and pulled her napkin into her lap. "Sounds like a hard life."

While they ate the scones, eggs benedict, fruit salad and whipped cream and strawberry-covered waffles, Leo explained her first mission to meet with Olvadi.

When she was done explaining the correspondence and the appointments that she had around the city to partake in a number of events on behalf of the mayor, Minny wasn't thinking that it was the easy way to make a living.

"So, why is this place called the Night Garden?"

"Oh, the plants glow at night. There are different flowers that bloom in the dark. It is really quite lovely." Leo got up. "I will be right back."

She walked into the manor and found the kitchen. Lima was sitting and reading a magazine that featured Leo and Matthias on the cover. Leo shook that off.

"Lima?"

"Yes, Ms. Wicks?"

"Thank you so much for lunch. May I hug you?"

Lima hopped down and grinned. "I would love that."

Leo hugged the chef and felt better for the contact. "Minny and I loved it."

"She is welcome anytime."

"Thanks for all you do. It means a lot that I don't have to go hunting for food."

"My pleasure."

Leo thanked her again and left her, going in search of her sister.

Minny was in the maze. "Damn it, Minny!"

"Uh, Leo, I think I need some help." Her voice sounded behind the hedges.

Leo went through the maze, grabbed her sister by the hand and hauled her out.

"How did you find me so fast?"

"I could smell you. You smell sort of like me and a bit like milk. Come on, Melly will be getting hungry."

Leo walked her sister through the manor and out the front door.

"I don't need a force-march home, Leo."

"You do need it if you don't want to lactate all over your shirt. My guess is that you have three minutes until you turn into Niagara Falls."

Minny may have been perturbed, but she picked up her pace. They made it through the door and over to where the baby had just started wailing.

Leo watched her sister with the baby and Leela in the background getting to the laundry now that Minny was home. It was nice to see everyone out in the light with no fear striking through her.

Leo had taken care of one issue, and Matthias had taken care of the other. If the XIA took care of the demon issue, it would wrap up all the issues begun on her first week as the mayor's assistant.

Instinct told her that the demands of the job were always going to run neck and neck with the rewards. At least she had a while to work out what she wanted after Melly graduated. She didn't want to admit that it was Matthias.

epilogue

Leo raised her glass. "Ladies and gentlemen, I am happy to be able to announce the graduation of my niece Melody and her entry into the Mage Guild. Congratulations, Melly, you and your hard work have gotten you this far, I have no doubt that they will take you to limits I can't imagine. To Melody Wicks!"

The ballroom of the manor was filled with people who raised their glasses and toasted, "Melody Wicks!"

Melody walked over and hugged her. "Aunty Leo. You haven't aged a day."

Matthias came up behind them. "That would be my fault. Congratulations, Melody. Consider this a gift from your aunt and myself."

He extended one of the parchment envelopes that he was known for.

Melody blushed. "You didn't have to, Uncle Matthias."

"I am aware of that, but these events need to be celebrated. Life passes quickly if you don't mark the occasions. Speaking of which, Leonora, would you come with me into the gardens?"

"Of course, Matthias." She put her hand on his arm, and she wiggled her fingers at a few friendly faces.

They walked out of the room, and Minny was there with her partners. She had left the rest of her six children at home.

Leo looked at her curiously as Matthias led her to the entry to the maze. He knelt and she blushed. It usually was a prelude to something not suitable for public viewing.

"Leonora Wicks, years ago you came to me and asked me for help, promising everything short of your life in exchange for my help. I gave you that help, and now, we are at the end of our contract."

She inhaled sharply as he pulled out a box that twisted open to reveal another piece of heartstone. She held her breath when he took her hand.

"Leonora, will you marry me and be my bride, my partner and my companion in all things?"

Leo looked over to Minny, who was standing with her thumbs up.

Melody was in the doorway, and she nodded, flapping her hand toward Leo.

Leo frowned. "Can I be your partner without marrying you?"

He blinked. "Of course."

"Do I still get the ring?"

He laughed. "You do."

"Then, yes, I will marry you." She laughed, and he put the ring on her left hand. It fit, and she suspected that Dorn had had something to do with that.

She leaned down and kissed him, bowling him

back into the grass. She heard Melody laughing, and Minny snorted as she rolled the Mayor of Redbird City around in the grass until the kiss turned from playful into something far more serious.

When he raised his head so she could breathe, he smiled. "Now, we get to enjoy the engagement party."

She yelped as he hauled her to her feet and pulled her back in front of their friends and family for the announcement.

She was hugged, congratulated and a portrait of the engaged couple was unveiled.

Leo covered her eyes as she got a load of the image of her bent over Matthias's arm while the crimson gown was edged as low as it could go without obscenity. Matthias's fangs were exposed and descending to her breast. They were the cover of a romance novel rendered in oil.

Matthias had amusement dancing in his gaze. "It is going to be the cover of all the gossip magazines tomorrow morning with the announcement of our engagement."

She whirled on him. "You didn't!"

"I did. It will make an impression and be a collector's item."

The crowd was laughing and admiring the image, and Leo didn't know why she had let Matthias convince her to pose for it. The other fifty images had ranged from decorous to dangerous, but this had been the only outright goofy one.

She tapped the Heart of Life around her neck, and she glared up at him. "I will find a way to exact my revenge."

He grinned. "I look forward to it. We will have centuries for you to get your revenge."

She paused and sighed. "It is a hilarious picture, but you know some of the vampire kings won't like it."

"Let them bring their complaints to me. I haven't put down an uprising in decades."

"Aw, I love it when you are bossy." She grabbed his tie and pulled him down to her, kissing him wildly.

When she let him lift his head, he whispered, "Then, dearest, you love me all the time."

"Yes, but I am sure that it will wear off to a mild affection in a few centuries."

She stroked his cheek, and he leaned into her touch, just as he had since their first anniversary. It was one thing that time hadn't changed, and she hoped that it never would. Leo had put him off long enough; tonight, she would cease defying eternity and let it take her into the next phase of her existence. And then, she would jump him.

Author's Note

Well, not as much interaction with the other books as I thought, but she met Benny and the boys.

In the next book, *Monster Baiter,* we deal with Sophia's peculiar curse and how it creates love-life issues when you constantly look underage.

Sophia drives out to lonely roads and woods where folks have been disappearing, and she does what she is best at. She becomes the bait.

Thanks for reading,
Viola Grace

About the Author

Viola Grace (aka Zenina Masters) is a Canadian sci-fi/paranormal romance writer with ambitions to keep writing for the rest of her life. She specializes in short stories because the thrill of discovery, of all those firsts, is what keeps her writing.

An artist who enjoys a story that catches you up, whirls you around and sets you down with a smile on your face is all she endeavours to be. She prefers to leave the drama to those who are better suited to it, she always goes for the cheap laugh.

Made in the USA
Charleston, SC
28 May 2016